"Would you lik[e]

"Huh?" CJ swallowed. He hadn't held a little one since Harper's babysitting days, and he'd made the baby cry.

"She won't break. Promise," Harper said.

"Um… Okay." He extended his arms, hands up. Muscles tensing, he waited for her to place Emaline in the crook of his bent elbows.

"Relax and hold her to you."

He did. Then warmth and an odd paternal pull washed over him as he cradled her soft little body against his chest.

Making a gurgling noise, she bounced, her arm smacking him in the face before her fist found her mouth.

Peering down at her, he laughed. "That must taste awfully good. Think I can get a nibble?" He brought her other hand to his lips and mouthed it, eliciting a giggle. "Just one more bite?" He did it again, unable to contain his grin. He glanced at Harper, his attention snagged by the intensity in her eyes.

She was looking at him with the same expression, the same focus, as she often had, back when they'd been dating.

Jennifer Slattery is a writer and speaker who has addressed women's and church groups across the nation. As the founder of Wholly Loved Ministries, she and her team help women rest in their true worth and live with maximum impact. When not writing, Jennifer loves spending time with her adult daughter and hilarious husband. Visit her online at jenniferslatterylivesoutloud.com to learn more or to book her for your next women's event.

Books by Jennifer Slattery

Love Inspired

Restoring Her Faith
Hometown Healing
Building a Family
Chasing Her Dream
Her Small-Town Refuge
Falling for the Family Next Door
Recapturing Her Heart

Visit the Author Profile page at LoveInspired.com.

Recapturing
Her Heart

Jennifer Slattery

LOVE INSPIRED
INSPIRATIONAL ROMANCE

LOVE INSPIRED®
INSPIRATIONAL ROMANCE

PLEASE RECYCLE

THIS PRODUCT IS RECYCLABLE

Recycling programs for this product may not exist in your area.

ISBN-13: 978-1-335-59869-1

Recapturing Her Heart

Copyright © 2024 by Jennifer Slattery

All rights reserved. No part of this book may be used or reproduced in any manner whatsoever without written permission except in the case of brief quotations embodied in critical articles and reviews.

This is a work of fiction. Names, characters, places and incidents are either the product of the author's imagination or are used fictitiously. Any resemblance to actual persons, living or dead, businesses, companies, events or locales is entirely coincidental.

For questions and comments about the quality of this book, please contact us at CustomerService@Harlequin.com.

Love Inspired
22 Adelaide St. West, 41st Floor
Toronto, Ontario M5H 4E3, Canada
www.LoveInspired.com

Printed in U.S.A.

And now abideth faith, hope, charity, these three; but the greatest of these is charity.
—*1 Corinthians* 13:13

To my father-in-law John Slattery.
I was blessed to know you.

Chapter One

Clammy hands gripping her steering wheel, Harper Moore forced herself to park in front of the one place in Sage Creek, Texas, she had determined to avoid. The name painted on the dusty window—Nuts, Bolts and Boards—seemed to mock her, reminding her of the words she'd spoken the night she and CJ Jenkins broke up.

She'd never intended to hurt him. She'd simply wanted more than this town and, by association, CJ could offer.

Yet here she was, back home, living with her mom, no less, and needing help from the people least likely to give it to her. But only for a season. God willing, in two months, she'd move with her daughter and return to the world of professional dance.

But first, she needed to muster the courage to get out of her car, march into the Jenkinses' hardware store and apply for a job.

Her baby's paternal grandmother, Cynthia Rhodam, Managing Director of South East Repertory, had promised to use her connections to land Harper a prestigious choreographer position. As if that could rectify the injustice Harper suffered when the woman forced her to resign to avoid tarnishing her son's name. Nor could a job, however needed, heal the wound caused when Chaz denied paternity.

Harper could've fought the matter. She'd certainly had every right. But standing up to someone with such influence could've killed any future opportunities in the dance world.

Lost child support, she could handle. The death of her dream, she could not. So, she'd conceded to "lie low" until lawyers resolved a sexual harassment suit against Emaline's father that didn't directly involve Harper but affected her nonetheless.

Needing a dose of encouragement, she called her best friend.

Trisha answered on the first ring. "Hey, girl. Been praying for you. How'd it go?"

She released a sigh. "Haven't done the deed yet."

"Okay. What do you need from me?"

"A reminder that I can do hard things? If only I'd been able to make ends meet in Seattle." Unfortunately, childcare fees and the skyrocketed cost of living had forced her home.

"But then you wouldn't get to see me."

Harper laughed. "You do remember this is temporary, right? Just until I save funds for first and last on an apartment and a month's worth of childcare fees."

"And assuming Chaz's mother holds true to her word?"

"And that." Emaline's paternal grandmother hadn't exactly demonstrated high integrity. But she did hold a lot of influence in the dance industry. "If only the library would give me more hours, I wouldn't have to be here, about to eat the biggest slice of humble pie imaginable."

"You've got nothing to feel insecure about. March in there with your head high. And remember, you look amazing, by the way."

Sitting taller, Harper eyed her reflection in the rearview mirror, more thankful than ever that her beautician friend had treated her to a free hair makeover. "I do love the burgundy highlights."

"I knew they'd look great with your sable-toned locks. Like I said yesterday, the color combo really makes your blue eyes pop."

"Thanks." The curl cream she'd purchased, which emitted a faint pineapple-coconut scent, countered the Texas humidity that normally turned her wavy hair to frizz.

Regardless, she couldn't help but view herself

through CJ's eyes, certain she'd find nothing but bitterness and contempt staring back at her.

"You want to celebrate with milkshakes at Wilma's after?" Trisha asked.

"Can't. Promised Mom I'd clean the kitchen in exchange for her watching Emaline."

While her mother hadn't always been the best source of support, and often offered it with contempt, Harper was grateful for her help now.

Unfortunately, her father hadn't been a part of her life since he bailed on her and her mom fifteen years prior.

She released a heavy breath that did little to ease her churning gut. "Guess I best get this over with." Ending the call, she grabbed her printed résumé and stepped out and into the pleasant spring sun. The soft scent of geraniums and petunias wafted toward her from pots hanging from either side of the lamppost streetlight. The faint twang of a country song emanated from the hardware store, merging with the eighties' rock drifting from the adjacent pawnshop.

Harper paused on the sidewalk to center herself, watching through the window as Nancy, CJ's mom, spoke with a potbellied man wearing a stretched-out navy T-shirt. Harper scanned the store's interior for a glimpse of CJ's dad, John Michael. She'd much prefer to deal with him. With his relatively even-keeled personality, he was less likely to respond to Harper's job inquiry with venom.

Nancy, however, epitomized the mama-bear sweatshirt she used to wear. Hopefully time had overcome any residual anger. CJ's mom was an adult, after all. And a business owner, one who, if that Help Wanted sign tacked to the window still held true, needed an employee.

"Are you going in?" The deep voice startled her.

She turned toward the tall, lanky man who held the door open for her. "Yes, thank you." Her legs and fingers felt tingly as she stepped inside, and not from the gush of air-conditioning blowing overhead.

Nancy shifted in their direction. "Welcome to—" Her instant smile faltered before returning, taut, below stony eyes. Her gaze remained locked on Harper.

"Ma'am." Her lungs felt tight as she fought for the courage to say why she'd come. Instead, Harper stared, mouth dry, at the woman who'd once encouraged her to call her Mama, while Nancy stared back.

An approaching customer wanting a particular color of paint interrupted the heavy silence that stretched between them. Watching Nancy disappear down a nearby aisle, Harper released the breath she'd been holding.

Everything within her urged her to exit the store as quickly as possible. Instead, she squared her shoulders and walked, stiff-legged, toward the long, pine checkout counter.

What would she do if, once Nancy returned, she kicked her out? At least the store was nearly empty; any public humiliation wouldn't gather much of an audience. Not that she expected Nancy to respond with such unprofessional behavior. She could, however, see the woman avoiding her until Harper's growing anxiety overpowered the last of her resolve.

"Yes, ma'am. We've got two-wheel dollies next to our moving boxes."

Harper froze, a jolt shooting through her, at the sound of CJ's approaching voice. She darted behind a steel pillar barely wider than her five-foot-four frame.

What was he doing here? Her friend Trisha had seen him scraping paint off somebody's shed not long ago. They'd assumed he was working construction, but he may have been helping a friend. Or, maybe, like her, he needed to piece together the hours from two jobs to make ends meet.

Harper focused on his conversation with his customer to gauge which direction they were heading.

"My friends keep pestering me to hire a moving company to come in and pack all my things."

The woman huffed. "As if I've got money for that." Her footsteps halted. "Oh. Spackle. Is this what I need to fill in the holes in my walls? From hanging picture frames and such?"

It sounded as if she and CJ had stopped a few feet away. Unfortunately, they appeared in no hurry to leave. Harper held her breath as the woman went on to talk about her various collections and other items she hoped to sell at a garage sale. Apparently, she was moving into an assisted-living facility near her oldest son.

"That sounds like a big transition." Compassion softened CJ's tone, his words unhurried, as if prepared to listen for as long as the lady needed.

He'd always been kind, a trait that had initially caught her off guard. She'd expected him, the high school quarterback, to act cocky and self-obsessed. Instead, he'd been the first to reach out to the new kid or the teen lingering on the fringe. Although she'd initially felt drawn to his striking good looks, it was his heart that had captured hers.

She could still envision his easy grin and the way his greenish-gray eyes lit whenever they landed on hers.

Had he changed much over the years?

Harper waited until CJ and his customer's conversation and footfalls receded, then slipped out from behind the pillar. Curiosity and something she couldn't name drew her in the direction of their voices. Second to the last aisle to the end, she paused, pulse quickened, and slowly peered around the corner.

CJ stood with his back to her, talking to a short lady with long silver hair and a boxy torso. His faded blue jeans complemented his muscular frame, and his broad shoulders seemed to strain against the cotton of his teal T-shirt. He wore his hair shorter than he had in high school. The blond locks that used to curl up from under his cowboy hat were not presently visible.

He laughed at something the woman said— Harper couldn't quite make it out.

"Well, now, we can't let that happen." He handed his customer a roll of Bubble Wrap and a stack of large flattened boxes. "My folks would never let me hear the end of it. Anything else you need?"

She shook her head and the two turned in Harper's direction—CJ's widening eyes landing on her before she could dart out of sight. Thick brows pinched together, he frowned, seeming at a loss for words. But then he gave a quick firm nod she'd seen him greet others with numerous times before.

The steady thud of his boots matched the loud pounding of her heart as, expression tense, he strolled toward her. "Harper."

"Hey, CJ." Her voice came out squeaky.

The customer followed his eyes, and a look of curiosity flashed across her face. She offered Harper a smile and thanked CJ for his help. "I best get back home to wrap those gnomes I told you about."

His chuckle sounded forced. "You do that. And don't forget to call Pastor Roger to ask about borrowing Trinity Faith's cargo trailer. He'd be thrilled to know it was being put to good use, as long as he hasn't already promised it to someone else that day."

"I'll do that." The woman walked away with a wiggly fingered wave.

CJ's jaw muscle twitched as he faced Harper, his cedar-citrus aroma scenting the space between them. "You need help with something?" His tone carried an edge.

Although they'd seen one another around town about half a dozen times since she'd returned to Sage Creek, they'd managed to avoid each other until now. The downward slant of his flattened lips verified he wasn't any happier to break that trend than she was.

She rubbed the back of her arm. Clearly, Nancy wasn't the most challenging Jenkins family member to have this conversation with. "Do you work here?" If so, they'd be spending a great deal of time together.

Just how badly did she need this job?

Unfortunately, very.

The crevice between his brows deepened. Jutting his chin, he nodded. "No surprise there, huh?"

She winced inwardly, thinking about the words she'd spoken the night they broke up—how she'd told him that she wanted more, thereby implying that he, and the life he'd offered her, wasn't enough.

He studied her, a shadow of sorrow softening his glare. "I need to get back to work." He turned to leave.

"Wait." She grabbed his wrist, and a familiar shiver shot through her.

His frown returned. "What do you need, Harper?"

She couldn't remember him ever having spoken to her so harshly. Much had changed—because of her.

"I…" She pushed at her thumb cuticle. "Are your parents still hiring?"

"Why? You know of someone looking for a job?"

"Yeah. Me." She spoke quickly, before she could chicken out.

His eyebrows shot up, and he gave his head a slight shake, as if he wasn't sure he'd heard her correctly. "Aren't you working at the library?"

"I am, but they cut my hours." She'd been part-time since Christmas.

He sighed and scrubbed a hand over his face, probably contemplating the most professional way to brush her off. "Applications are in the office. Come on." He made a sweeping motion with his arm.

Sucking in a breath to still her jittery stomach, she followed him past a bin of screws, a ladder attached to a ceiling rail, like one might see in old libraries, and a large yellow barrel filled with rakes, prongs up.

At the back of the store, she lingered in the short hallway, beside a corkboard covered with community event posters and various flyers. Someone had German shepherd puppies for sale. Someone else was offering housecleaning services. Tomorrow, the church was hosting a craft bazaar and family carnival event to fund a youth-group mission trip. According to the thumbtacked page, the activities included face painting, a clown making balloon animals, a petting zoo and a bounce house, among other things.

CJ nudged a plastic cooler out of his way to reach a metal filing cabinet. The top drawer opened with a screech. He handed her a printed application. "You can fill this out now or take it home and bring it back."

Focused on the paper, she nodded. "Thank you." The question was, if she left, would she have the courage to return?

Christopher James Jenkins's steps felt stiff as he walked Harper to the break room. His gut was filled with the same ache he'd experienced the night she'd shattered his heart. Apparently, he hadn't healed as much as he'd thought in the five years since. That also meant her working here was a bad idea.

But he couldn't just turn her away without at least glancing at her application. He wasn't an expert in civil law, but it seemed that would qualify as job discrimination or something.

He motioned for her to sit at the scratched and wobbly table centering the space. "Can I get you a water or cup of coffee?"

She perched on the edge of a folding chair. "I'm fine, but thank you."

Lingering a few feet away, he watched as she leaned over the page. Her dark, wavy hair spilled forward, exposing the gentle curve of her slender neck. Her trim dancer's build from high school had filled out and softened in all the right ways.

He still caught his breath when her blue eyes, framed by thick, dark lashes, latched on to his. The vulnerability her nervous posture and heart-shaped face had displayed moments ago stirred emotions within him he'd thought had long died.

That she triggered a reaction at all, especially since she'd made it clear how little she'd thought of him, caused his teeth to clench.

Why was she here? Clearly, the life in the big city she'd left him for hadn't been enough to keep her attention, either.

Was it wrong that the thought gave him a measure of satisfaction?

With a mental shake, he crossed to the counter, gathered three days' worth of dirty mugs and tidied up the napkins and creamers. He picked up a damp rag next to the sink and wiped a splotch of ketchup from the countertop.

He cast a glance over his shoulder. "My folks can't pay much more than minimum wage. And they're looking for someone able to work evenings and weekends." He figured that alone would deter her.

She met his gaze. "I understand."

Hadn't that been one of her biggest fears? That she'd end up chained to this place—the store and town—forever? At least, that's how Trisha had later relayed it. She'd said Harper couldn't marry a man with zero ambition.

"CJ?" His mom's voice preceded her. "Harper." She stood in the doorway, her tone as cold as her expression. She moved to the table and glanced at the application. Her eyebrows plummeted. "You're looking for work?"

Harper's pen paused midstroke. "Yes, ma'am. If you and Mr. Jenkins will have me." Her voice trembled slightly.

His mom's gaze shot to CJ, her expression clouded, before landing back on Harper. "I see." She hesitated, as if contemplating saying more.

Remembering how stirred up his mother had been when he'd told her of the breakup, he hoped she wouldn't. His mom was anything but even-tempered, especially when someone hurt those she loved. And her stony expression suggested bitterness from that day still lingered.

He understood that. Whoever'd said time healed all wounds had never loved, and lost, a woman like Harper. The years had merely tamed the ache—a hurt he had no intentions of experiencing again.

Making eye contact, his mom tilted her head toward the door.

He nodded and followed her into the hall.

Arms crossed, Nancy stood with her back to the long plastic PVC sheets from the loading area entrance. "What's this about?"

"Don't know. Maybe she saw the Help Wanted sign in the window."

"We don't need help that badly."

"I agree."

Her gaze flicked back to the break room, and she frowned. "But she must be really struggling financially to come in here. And she does have a kid. That matters, regardless of how we all feel about her."

CJ's gut sank. "What are you saying?"

"That we need to pray on this some."

He didn't want to hear any talk about loving his enemies or giving them the shirt off his back. Harper had already taken too much.

His mom's phone chimed a text, and she glanced at the screen then at CJ. "Dad's asking for more information on those website plug-ins you told us about."

"Meant to work on that this morning." He'd poked around on a few websites but preferred to speak with an actual person. "I got sidetracked helping a gal find a tool for her father's birthday." If they wanted the store to survive this internet era, where folks were used to doing most of their shopping with a click, they'd need to provide on-line ordering options.

His folks disagreed, but they were willing to hear him out. They probably understood that he had additional reasons for wanting to expand their online presence. He needed to find a way to increase his exposure as an artist if he wanted to turn what his father called a "hobby" into a viable career. He wouldn't abandon his parents to run this place on their own. But adding another worker would allow him to reduce his hours since they hadn't yet been able to convince their part-time guy to increase his.

A steady crew would help his parents to maintain a more reasonable schedule as well. Their aging bodies wouldn't keep up with their seventy-plus-hour, highly physical workweeks forever. The way CJ saw it, every win for the store was a win for him, and vice versa.

But he'd much rather hire someone—anyone— other than Harper.

"I best go water our spring flowers." His mom bit off a hangnail. "When the ballerina princess is finished with her application, place it on my desk. Then walk her out."

"Okay."

He returned to the break room to find Harper waiting where he'd left her, typing on her phone.

She sprang to her feet when he entered. "Here." She handed him her completed paper.

He skimmed her work history with a raised brow. So, she had found her big break, after all. She'd worked for some Seattle-based dance company for just under a year. Why had she left? Had they cut her loose once she became pregnant? He doubted that was legal.

"Everything look okay?"

CJ glanced up to find her watching him with

a wrinkled brow. "Yeah. This is great." He motioned to the door then followed her out.

"When do you think y'all will make a decision?" Her tone conveyed a hint of anxiety.

"Soon. We're heading into our busy season." The uptick should have started with the coming of spring. But while their sales numbers had increased, it had not been by as much as his parents had hoped. They feared they were losing people to a new chain that had popped up in the next county. CJ doubted locals would drive that far for lumber and nails. Contractors, however, were another matter. Still, he had to believe the fact that they'd always charged fair prices would count for something.

"Oh, wow." Harper stopped in front of a section his dad had allowed CJ to use to display some of his chain-saw carvings. He'd marked off the corner area using a wooden arch made of two thick trunks, bark shining with finishing wax. She gazed up at his name burned into the sign attached to the tops by adjacent chains. "Are these yours?"

Did he detect a note of admiration in her voice? Standing a mite taller, he nodded. "It relaxes me."

"Do you mind?" She stepped toward his designs.

"Not at all." He followed as she approached a carving of three bear cubs climbing a stripped branch.

"This is amazing."

CJ hated that her praise still affected him. "Thank you." He lingered in the center of the circular rug bearing a red Texas star as she moved from one carving to the next.

"I had no idea you were so creative." She paused in front of a baby fox standing in the center of a hollowed-out stump. "How long have you been doing this?"

About a year after Harper had left, CJ had learned from Trisha that his supposed lack of ambition had played a significant role in their breakup. Seeing him now, working in the same place that he always had, as she'd predicted, had probably confirmed her assessment.

She'd be wrong.

But…would Harper view his newfound passion for carving as him chasing a fantasy or an attainable dream?

Her opinion shouldn't matter.

He shifted his weight to his other foot. "A while."

He straightened a stack of promotional cards printed on glossy card stock. "Got into it a couple years ago after watching a demonstration in Branson."

He'd gone camping with some buddies shortly after his and Harper's breakup, devasted and forced to rethink how he'd envisioned the rest of his life playing out. For a while, he'd floundered without motivation for much of anything. When he'd learned how Harper had felt regarding his so-called lack of drive, his low aspirations had felt like a personal defect.

He now knew he simply hadn't yet discovered the thing that made him feel most alive.

CJ rested a hand on his belt buckle. "The town was hosting a Timber festival, with activities, live music, and various artists and craftsmen, chainsaw carvers included."

"Interesting."

"It was." He chuckled, remembering one man in particular dressed in jeans and a plaid flannel, his long, black hair pulled into one of those messy man-buns folks used to make social media memes out of. "About half the guys looked like they'd come from a remote mountain somewhere—with their wild eyebrows curling every which way and their mouths hidden behind bushy mustaches and beards."

"Not exactly the standard image of an artist, huh?"

"True." That was probably why those men had made such an impact. They'd helped him see that a guy could be creative and masculine. In this, they'd given him permission to explore an outlet he'd never previously considered. That experience had awakened a part of him he hadn't known existed. A love that felt so inherent to his being, he'd found himself wanting to downplay its intensity to shield himself from further rejection.

Shoulders stiff, he watched Harper peruse each item, a hint of a smile emerging as she paused over some of his most complex pieces.

And if her estimation of him had changed?

His heart squeezed, threatening to unleash emotions he'd spent the past five years fighting against. What was that saying about falling into the same trap twice?

But what if the sense of adventure that attracted her to Seattle had left her disappointed? What if she'd realized all that was lost the day she'd left, with the wisdom that can only come from shattered expectations, and had returned for good?

Chapter Two

The next morning, Harper woke early and was showered and ready to go by nine thirty. Behind her, Emaline, also dressed and ready, lay on her Noah's ark baby blanket, playing contentedly with the brightly colored animal rings dangling from the arch of her floor mat "gym." Considering Emaline's disrupted sleep the night before, she'd likely need a nap in an hour or two.

That could be a good thing, if it caused her to sleep through church. Not so much, if it made her fussy.

Harper, on the other hand, would need to fight to stay awake.

She scrutinized her reflection in the mirror, trying to remember what the women had been wearing the last time she'd attended Trinity Faith.

Business casual was probably the safest choice. She'd selected a peach dress with a gathered neckline decorated with buttons down the front. For shoes, she chose cream ankle-strap wedges.

She added a hint of gloss to her lips, fluffed her hair, then turned to her happily cooing daughter. "All right, sweet girl." She eased Emaline out from under her hanging mobile and kissed her cheek. "You ready to see how most people in this town spend their Sunday mornings? And hopefully show Mrs. Jenkins I'm not a terrible person?"

If she wanted to land that hardware store job, she needed to find a way to soften the woman's opinion of her. Hopefully, her seeing Harper sitting in the pews would help.

She cast a nervous glance to the ceiling. Was that a wrong reason to attend church?

With Emaline cradled close to her chest, Harper exited her room.

Her mom's voice drifted toward her. It sounded like she was on the phone.

Hearing her name, Harper stopped midstep to listen.

"I mean, I'm not exactly raking in the money, as you well know. Things have been tight. I had to call out quite a bit the past few months due to my back. Now my boss is threatening to fire me. Not that he's ever given me enough work to actually make a decent living." She huffed.

Who was her mom talking to?

"I'm going to talk to Harper. Tell her she needs to start paying rent. Maybe pitch in for food, too. The good Lord knows I could use the extra cash."

Harper's stomach dropped. How had she not realized how much her mother struggled?

But what could she do? She'd put in applications at about every business in Sage Creek, even those that said they weren't hiring on the chance that they might soon.

Regardless, she needed to contribute more financially. That was another reason she desperately needed Nancy to hire her. And, God willing, give her enough hours to allow her to pay rent, help with groceries and save up for a move to the city.

What if nothing came of the choreographer's job? Emaline's paternal grandmother—or father, for that matter—wasn't exactly a person of honor who kept her word.

Then she'd find something else—teaching private lessons or something.

For now, at least she received free babysitting. If that were to change, it'd probably cost more to work than she earned.

With a quick glance to her mother, who sat with her back to her in the living room, Harper dashed into the kitchen for a bagel and cup of coffee. Not that her jittery nerves needed the caffeine, but her sleep-deprived brain did.

She took a sip and winced. Lukewarm. Not the most appetizing, but it'd do.

Rounding the corner, she ran smack into her mom, dying the front of Harper's dress in a lovely shade of brown.

"Oh." Her mom stepped back. "Sorry about that."

"No big deal." She glanced at the carpet, thankful her clothes had absorbed the spill—for her and her mom's relationship.

As to Harper's wardrobe, however, that was another story.

Lovely. Now she was going to be late, especially considering this was her only wrinkle-free dress.

Did her mom even own an iron?

By the time she finally left, she felt more than a little frazzled and debated heading back inside. But she really needed that hardware store job. Now more than ever.

At the church, the parking lot was nearly full. The sun streaked through the clouds drifting past the bell tower and steeple. A stained-glass Gothic window, vibrant against the white siding, stood on either side of the door. Bordering the stone foundation, bluebonnets, pink buttercups and red poppies grew between neatly trimmed bushes.

Locking her car, she pressed her lips to the side

of her daughter's soft head and inhaled her sweet baby scent. "We've got this, right, baby girl?"

Why did she feel so nervous?

Because she hadn't stepped inside a church in five years and wasn't sure what to expect? Or because she was apprehensive about potentially running into Nancy, the woman she hoped to see but would also rather avoid?

Or because she might run into CJ?

Probably all three.

Squaring her shoulders, Harper strode across the asphalt, up the concrete stairs and through the heavy wooden doors. The air, cooler than outside but more humid nonetheless, emitted a musty aroma mixed with lemon-scented wood polish and an undercurrent of dust. Rich notes from an organ flowed over her as she stepped into the short foyer separating the entrance from the visible sanctuary beyond.

Great. As she feared, service had already started.

A few heads turned, surveying her as she stood, stiffly, beneath the archway. Others swayed to the music, led in song by a robed choir up front.

Wiping a sweaty hand on her skirt, Harper scanned the rows of heads in front of her. A balding man was fighting with a toddler determined to climb over the pew back.

Movement in her peripheral view caught her attention. She turned, inhaling sharply to see CJ walking toward her, a look of surprise in his eyes.

He was clean-shaven and dressed in a navy-and-white plaid collared shirt with pearl buttons and a silver buckle centered with a turquoise stone. It felt odd to see him without his cowboy hat, but then she remembered where they were. Back in high school, one of her friends used to joke that, with his strong jaw, blond hair, now spiked, and chiseled build, he belonged on the cover of one of those outdoorsman magazines.

If that was true then, it was triply so now.

He smelled like a mixture between leather, sage and apple. "Morning." His hoarse whisper made her feel as if she were disrupting the service.

Harper nodded with a shaky smile. "Hello." Why did her stomach feel so unsettled whenever he was around? Whereas he always seemed ultraconfident and completely unfazed.

As if she no longer meant anything to him.

And why would she? They hadn't dated in over five years.

His eyes softened as he looked briefly at Emaline, who'd shoved her fist into her mouth and was blowing raspberries. "Hey, cutie," he whispered, then looked at Harper. "Would you like me to walk you to the nursery?"

That was kind of him to offer. To notice she'd come in, period, and make an effort to see that she felt comfortable.

She bit her lip and scanned the sanctuary. Had anyone else brought in their baby?

Although she didn't see any infants, she noted a handful or so of children squirming about. A round-faced boy maybe nine years old was alternating between bouncing in his seat and staring awkwardly at a couple behind him. Harper was half expecting the child to start making silly faces.

Harper bit the inside of her lip to stifle her laugh before turning back to CJ. "Would it be okay if I kept her with me?"

"Whatever makes you most comfortable." He handed her a bulletin from the stack on top of his Bible.

Ah. He served as an usher. That's why he was acting so helpful, not because he actually cared that she felt as out of place as a hip-hop dancer tossed onstage at *The Nutcracker*.

He guided her to an empty seat next to an older couple near the back right and pulled a thick green book from the pocket in front of her. "Page three seventy-eight." He opened it for her then handed it over as she slid into the row. "'I Surrender All.'"

She blinked. "You what?"

"The song." He tapped the title on the left-hand side.

"Oh. Right." Warmth climbed up her neck. "Thank you."

He nodded, studied her a moment, then walked away.

Spine straight, legs crossed at the ankles, she focused on the printed lyrics while casting furtive glances at the people singing around her. Nancy and her husband sat halfway up to the right, a family of four on one side and a younger couple on the other.

Swiveling slightly, she slid a look behind her. CJ occupied a wooden chair placed against the back wall. Was he seeing anyone? Considering the size of Sage Creek, seems she would've heard if he was.

Not that this was any of her business, except that she wanted to know he was happy.

His gaze landed on hers. Face hot once again, Harper turned back around, gently swaying Emaline to sleep while frantically scanning the printed lyrics to catch up. By the time she figured out that the congregation had moved to another song entirely, the pastor was walking onto the stage while the choir streamed off.

His message was on identity, and he repeated the phrase, "You got to know who you are and whose you are," about half a dozen times. "Ain't no one else has the right to define you or tell you what you're worth."

"That's right!" a male voice from the right boomed, startling Harper.

She scanned the parishioners, unsettled to find Nancy watching her with an unreadable expression. Upon eye contact, the woman straightened and turned back around.

Was she as surprised as CJ had clearly been to see Harper there? And if so, was that a good thing?

If it got her the job, yes.

Maybe Harper should try to talk to her after church. Not about the job, by any means. That would be all sorts of impolite. She'd simply say hi and hopefully create some positive interactions to counter whatever negative emotions the woman felt toward her.

When the service ended, she held Emaline close and filed out behind an older man with a black comb-over and protruding ears. The line bottlenecked at the archway as people chatted with one another. Someone's overpowering floral perfume and the increased noise combined with her growing sleepiness, threatening to give Harper a headache.

She glanced from the chair CJ had been sitting in to behind her to catch a glimpse of Nancy through the throng. She stood at the end of her row talking to a larger woman wearing a fuchsia blouse.

"Harper!"

Recognizing the enthusiastic voice, she turned toward her friend with a smile. "Trisha, hi."

"Why didn't you tell me you were coming? I would've saved you a seat."

Because Harper had reserved the right, up until she'd ascended the church steps, to change her mind. But she blamed her lack of communication on her daughter. "I wasn't sure how Emaline would do. If we'd actually be able to stay." That wasn't entirely false.

They stepped aside so as not to block traffic.

"Boy, do I hear that." Trisha tucked her bulletin into her Bible. "Come with me to get my munchkins?"

"Uh…" She looked back at Nancy, still engaged in conversation. Oh, well. At least she'd seen Harper there. That had to count for something.

Harper still felt guilty over her motivations for attending. She glanced at the ceiling. *I'll come again—to learn more about You next time.*

And if You help me get that job at Nuts, Bolts and Boards, I'll be here every Sunday.

* * *

After service, CJ's friend Oliver snagged him to offer a business proposition. "My landlord wants to sell my building. Asked if I wanted to buy it. Said he's giving me first dibs before listing it."

"And?"

"I would if he was willing to divide it up and let me purchase the area I run my antique store in. But I don't need, nor can I afford, the whole space. You still wanting to open a gallery of sorts to sell your chain-saw carvings?"

"Eventually."

"Any way I can get you to move the needle in the sooner rather than later direction?" He relayed the price and about how much they'd need to put down.

CJ whistled. "That's a lot. A good deal, I'm sure. But more than I've got."

"Think you can wrangle up some funds, maybe liquidate some of your bigger pieces?"

"The idea's appealing. It's the doing that'll be the challenge. So far, I haven't done a great job of getting my work to sell with any kind of consistency."

"This might-could give you the motivation you need." Oliver clamped a hand on his shoulder. "Just think about it."

"Will do."

His friend helped him gather dropped bulletins to be tossed and return Bibles to the back of pews.

"I saw you talking to Harper earlier." Oliver picked up a pacifier lying on the floor. "Y'all patch things up?"

CJ tensed. "We don't hate each other, if that's what you mean."

"That's progress."

"And about as far as things will progress."

Oliver laughed then left CJ to finish up and turn off the sanctuary lights.

The sun streamed through the stained glass, decorating the wood flooring in beams of red, blue and green. Nearing the heavy double doors that, now closed, separated the large open space from the foyer, he paused midstep at the sound of Harper's familiar laugh.

He closed his eyes as a wave of sorrow swept over him, followed by a rush of anger at the fact that, after all these years, his heart still felt so bruised. It'd be so easy to talk his mom out of hiring her, if only to retain the distance he and Harper had managed to keep between one another since her return. But he also wanted to do right by God.

The Bible said not to withhold good when a fella had the power to act. As much as he'd like to believe otherwise, he figured the proverb applied in this instance. Besides, as his mom had said, Harper had a kid. The baby certainly wasn't to blame for his pain any more than she was for the circumstances that had brought her mama back. Didn't seem right for the cutie to bear the consequences, either.

Someone's phone chimed a notification. A voice, sounded like Trisha St. James's, followed. "I better get back to my poor, sick husband, who clearly has the worst head cold in the history of all mankind." Sarcasm deepened her tone.

With a deep breath, he strode forward, reaching the concrete steps moments after Harper and her friend, now in the parking lot, had separated, each to their respective vehicles.

Once at his truck, he was surprised to see Harper's car still in the lot. Seeing her with her baby this morning, the tender way she'd spoken to her, and the way Emaline had smiled and babbled in return, caused a wave of grief to swell within him. He'd always thought Harper would make a great mom. Seemed his hunch had been right. He'd also assumed he'd be able to see the nurturing side of her bloom, day in and day out, as they'd raised children together.

Giving himself a mental shake, he slid into his driver's seat, slipped on his sunglasses and turned his key in the ignition. One of his favorite country music songs poured through his radio, and the scent of stale coffee wafted from the half-filled mug he'd left in his cup holder.

About to turn onto B Street, he cast one last glance at Harper through his rearview mirror. She was still sitting, parked, in her vehicle. Based on the way she smacked her steering wheel, she was *not* happy. Engine problems? Not exactly something a single mom on a part-time, and likely minimum wage, salary needed. On the most inconvenient day to boot, considering Sage Creek's lone mechanic didn't work or answer his phone most Sundays.

Then again, she could always call someone else.

Although everything within him longed to pretend he hadn't seen her, manners dictated he at least check that she was okay, especially considering he served on the church's greeting team. With a heavy exhale, he shifted into Reverse and looped back around.

Her blush was evident as, window down, he idled his vehicle beside hers. "You all right?"

Her thin eyebrows pinched together, and her gaze seemed to falter, as if she were debating how to answer. She never had liked asking for help. That probably made her current predicament, finance-wise, all the more challenging.

It must have taken a great deal of courage and

humility for her to walk into his parents' store. Jolted by her presence or not, he respected that.

She looked at her baby, who'd begun to fuss, then back at him with a sheepish smile. "My car won't start."

He nodded, parked and got out. A faint floral scent wafted toward him as he neared her car. "Give it a try so I can hear it."

She did. The engine made one click and nothing more.

The lights in the car were on, so it wasn't the battery. Didn't look like an issue with her anti-theft immobilizer; the vehicle's computer seemed to be working. "Probably an issue with your starter."

She now stood outside her vehicle, gently swaying, daughter clutched to her chest. "Is that expensive to fix?"

He shrugged. "Maybe three hundred fifty?"

"Okay, thanks. Guess I better call a tow truck, huh?"

"Doubt you'll reach anyone today."

"Right." Either the sun was making her eyes water, or she was fighting tears. "Thank you for your help." She grabbed her phone from the seat in her car, probably to call her folks.

"Hop in my truck and I'll give you a ride home."

"Are you sure?"

Having Harper sitting close beside him, her

vulnerability making her even more beautiful than the day she broke his heart? That was the last thing he wanted. Regardless of their past, he wasn't jerk enough to walk away.

"It's no problem." He opened her back passenger door, unhooked the car seat, and grabbed it and the diaper bag from the floorboard. "I was heading that way. Promised my mom I'd swing by the grocery for milk and butter on the way to Sunday supper."

"Thanks."

He nodded. "The baby's car seat okay, the pickup not having a back seat and all?"

"Yeah. So long as it's rear facing."

Minding his manners, he waited until both mother and child were securely settled inside the cab. Then he closed her door, rounded the front of his truck and slid behind the wheel.

With how her nearness sent his heart thudding, he was grateful for the barrier the infant and her bulky car seat formed between them. Seemed his heart was forgetting what his mind refused to let go—Harper had left him years ago, without so much as a backward glance.

He eased his truck onto the quiet residential street lined with well-manicured lawns and brick homes tucked behind cheery flower beds. Most of the houses had covered porches, some with rockers, others with wooden swings. The road dimmed as thick white clouds moved across the sun, then brightened again.

He stopped at a four-way. "What'd you think of the service?" He'd not seen her in church since they were kids and figured she hadn't been in some time.

"It wasn't nearly as long as I remembered. Guess that's a sign of age, huh? When an hour actually feels like an hour?"

An elementary-aged boy in jeans and a base-ball cap rode his bike down the sidewalk while two preschoolers raced big-wheels up and down a nearby driveway.

He gave a slight nod. "Guess so." A woman in all pink, from her shorts to her ball cap, jogged by. "And the sermon?" The pastor's message had been a bit mushier than he preferred—more "assurance" than action-focused. Yet he could see how the content might have encouraged Harper.

"It gave me some things to think about."

He wanted to ask her what, but they no longer had the type of relationship that allowed for such conversations. There'd been a time when they'd talked about pretty much everything.

Everything except her decision to leave Sage Creek. She'd obviously been contemplating that action for some time, at least long enough to send out college applications and secure housing. Yet she hadn't said a thing to him—the person she'd supposedly loved "more than anyone in the world"—until her bags were packed.

If she had told him, how would he have responded?

He would've begged her to stay. That was probably why she'd kept so quiet. While that realization helped ease the bite of the bitterness that remained, it didn't excuse her behavior.

"I saw in the bulletin that the youth are still doing their annual talent show." She pulled a tube of lotion from her purse and squirted some on her hands, releasing the scent of cherry blossoms. "Made me think of that 'synchronized swimming' routine you and your buddies performed."

He shook his head. "We were such dorks."

"The skit was hilarious—your facial expressions especially. I still can't believe you lost to that Mick Jagger impersonation."

Her easy banter suggested their interaction wasn't as hard for her as it was for him—yet one more reminder of how easily she'd walked away all those years ago.

"We still got our pizza." He tried to match her casual tone. "Ricky's mom bought us two large Supremes—so we were good."

"I'd forgotten how food-motivated you were."

Harper had always been great at making small talk. The part of him that had worried their drive would feel awkward was grateful for this. The part of him trying to forget how much fun they used to have together, not so much.

But maybe this was good—the beginning of a new normal. Could they rebuild the friendship they'd once shared without him losing his heart?

Was that even something he wanted? To open himself for future hurt? No, thank you.

He at least needed to reach a place where he didn't feel like he was holding his breath whenever she was around.

He pulled into her mom's cracked driveway, feeling a sense of déjà vu as he surveyed the peeling paint and dandelion-infested yard. A layer of dust covered the windows, and weeds sprouted up from the sun-bleached mulch lining the walk. A partially broken flowerpot sat on the porch next to a pair of old tennis shoes.

He was struck by how much hadn't changed, and yet, how much had.

Engine idling, he shifted into Park, got out and hurried to open the door for her, waiting as she unfastened her daughter's car seat.

He took it, with the child secure, and the diaper bag from her. "I got it."

"Thank you."

"No problem."

He followed her up the sagging steps. They'd barely reached the stoop when the door swung open to reveal Harper's mom, her hair mussed and showing two-inch gray roots.

"Well, I'll be." She wore a stained T-shirt with remnants of screen-printed words too faded to make out. Eyebrows raised about as high as they could go, she looked from CJ to Harper then back to him. "Christopher James. I thought I recognized that truck."

"Ma'am." He tipped his hat at her.

"Come in, darlin'." She moved aside and motioned to her home's dim interior. "I was just about to make a batch of sweet tea."

"I appreciate the offer, ma'am, but I can't stay. My mama's got Sunday supper waiting."

Mrs. Moore's face fell. "Another time then."

He shifted toward Harper. "Hope Mike's able to get your car up and running no problem." He handed Harper the car seat, started to leave, then stopped. He could fix her vehicle easily enough, and for the cost of parts. Matter of fact, he probably would've already offered had she been any other single mom he'd encountered at the church.

Seemed hypocritical for him not to do the same for her.

He turned back around. "Listen. I can come work on your car tomorrow."

"Are you sure?" Thin lines etched across her delicate forehead.

"I've got a bit of time around midmorning."

"Thank you!" Her eyes lit up, adding to her beauty.

With a nod, he hurried back to his truck before the vise squeezing his chest showed on his face.

Chapter Three

The next morning, CJ stayed busy dealing with contractors. For a Monday, he was surprised at the steady flow of business. Was the uptick due to the advertising campaign he'd pushed for? He'd finally talked his parents into stepping into the twenty-first century to utilize social media. A few quick videos with remodeling ideas, followed by a series of related discounts, had brought in folks they hadn't seen for a while.

Unfortunately, only a handful of them had ventured far enough into the store to see his carvings. No one had purchased anything.

He'd never support himself as an artist this way.

With a sigh, he made his usual rounds to check what items they needed to reorder and what shelves needed tidying. Afterward, he popped into the office to ask his mom what she wanted him to prioritize—and to once again broach the conversation regarding Harper.

Alert to the irony of advocating for the woman who'd abandoned him, a twinge of bitterness contracted his muscles. But he refused to travel down that all-too-familiar road yet again. He'd fought much too hard to reclaim his joy and peace to forfeit it over a past offense.

He closed his eyes, asking God to cleanse his heart—a practice he'd learned from Pastor Roger.

Would this always be such a struggle?

"Hey, kiddo." His mom smiled as he stepped into the small, cluttered space.

Scribbled notes on random scraps of paper, various knickknacks, three mugs and a container of store-bought cookies covered most of her desktop. Family photos and framed drawings he'd made as a kid decorated the wall behind her.

"Hi." Slipping a hand in his pocket, he relayed the morning orders. "Our shipment of drywall arrived wet. We're going to have to scrap several pieces. Manufacturer's going to resend what we lost."

"Who was this for?"

"JK Interior Finishers." He rubbed the back of his neck.

"They're the ones working with that high-maintenance homeowner? The fella turning his garage into his man cave?"

"The guy who wanted it completed by yesterday. Unfortunately."

"Lovely." She typed on her computer keyboard.

Shifting his weight, he lingered then cleared his throat. "Have you and Dad made any decisions regarding Harper's application?"

"I don't want to talk about that now." Her typing became more forceful. She wiggled the mouse, clicked through a few things and paused. Her gaze landed on a flip-calendar to the right of her screen.

He followed her line of sight to the day's verse bordered with vines and flowers. It was from Proverbs 19:17, and read, "He that hath pity upon the poor lendeth unto the Lord; and that which he hath given will he pay him again."

That felt like a hard nugget to accept. "I've got to head out for a bit. Need me to do anything first?"

She looked at the clock above him and shook her head.

Ten minutes later, he found himself at Harper's house, fighting to suppress memories from all the nights, years ago, he'd dropped her off. He should've snagged Harper's number from her application to let her know he was coming. Better yet, had he asked for her car keys the day before, he could've fixed the thing with little interaction.

Yet here he was, parked in her driveway—which was empty.

If no one was home and the trip over had been a waste? Wouldn't hurt his feelings none. He could leave knowing he'd tried to do the right thing. A man couldn't do much more than that.

CJ stepped out, pocketed his keys and ambled up the walk to her stoop. He pressed the doorbell, waited, peered through slats caused by bends in the blinds and rang again. He turned to leave then stopped. He glanced about. Was that Harper—singing?

Seemed he'd be spending the rest of his morning turning a wrench, after all—a fact he'd feel good about if he were doing it for anyone else. It wasn't that he didn't want to help Harper. He did. At least, he *wanted* to want to help her.

Apparently, he had yet to conquer the resentment triggered by her leaving.

He followed the rise and fall of Harper's voice around the side of the house to the rusted chain-link fence bordering her backyard. The image of her dancing about while holding Emaline jolted him. Hair bouncing against her slender shoulders, Harper's face radiated joy as she gazed, completely enamored, at her daughter—who was equally enthralled with her mother.

"We shall go a-frolicking, up the hill and down again. Round and round and round again. Until we go to town again, on a spring sunshiny morning."

It sounded like one of the spontaneous songs she'd made up for the neighbor kids she used to babysit. When she'd thought no one else was within earshot. Once she'd caught him watching her. The blush in her cheeks and shy drop of her gaze had stirred something deep inside him.

She'd stolen his heart that night and stomped on it four years later. Seeing her tenderness with her daughter now felt like an elbow jab to the ribs—a vivid example of what could have been.

Yet she was here now. Did that change anything?

No. He hadn't been enough for her before. He had no desire to become her plan B now.

His phone rang, startling him.

Harper turned around, eyes wide, her face bearing the same expression and tinge of pink that had halted his breath years ago. Straightening, she smoothed back her breeze-stirred hair and walked toward him. "Hi."

He swallowed. "Hey."

His phone rang again.

"You going to get that?" she asked.

"Huh? Yeah." He glanced at the screen. It was his mom. Had he walked off with the forklift keys again? He patted his pockets. Nope. He answered. "Yes, ma'am?"

"About Harper… As much as I hate this, I know your father and I need to do the hard right thing. We want to set the example of how a person should act—to put feet to all those lessons we've given you over the years."

"You both have done nothing but demonstrate integrity."

"I appreciate you saying that, but I know I could've handled this situation better. My attitude has downright stunk. She needs a job, and she's got a little one to support. While she did you wrong, she was just a kid. As were you. Two teenagers caught up in a high school crush that, for a while, felt like the world. Clearly, the years have matured you both. Figure it's about time I start acting like a grown-up, too."

"Meaning?"

His mom ran hot at times, but she was always quick to admit when she'd been wrong. He admired that about her—even if her honorable choices negatively affected him.

Harper shot him periodic glances, listening but acting like she wasn't. She'd probably guessed why he'd come and was waiting to give him her keys.

His mom's breath vibrated through the phone. "I've decided to invite her in for an interview. Just wanted you to know."

"Okay." Oliver's offer to go in on that building, and therefore reduce the time spent at the store with Harper, was looking more appealing. It struck CJ as comical. They were hiring help, in part, so that he could focus on establishing himself as an artist, and if they hired Harper, she'd push him out even faster. He just needed to figure out how to earn his part of the down payment. "When were you thinking?"

"Soon as she can come in. We need the help, and obviously, she could use the money. I'll call her now and will text you whatever time we land on."

"I can ask. I'm with her now."

Harper's furtive glances became more direct. Watching him, she meandered over and lingered on the other side of the fence, carrying a faint scent of cinnamon with her.

"You're where?" Surprise hiked his mom's tone.

He rubbed a hand over his face and explained why he'd come. "Didn't feel right leaving her to pay for a tow and whatnot, when I can get it working." Prior to carving, he'd fiddled some with engine rebuilding. "Seems this morning might be as good a time as any, seeing how I'm already over here and all."

His mom didn't respond right away. When she did, her voice sounded flat. "I'm available now."

"I'll shoot you a text in a few."

He ended the call and slipped his phone into his back pocket. "You free for the next hour or so? For a job interview?"

Her eyes widened and then brightened with her smile. "Really? That would be great!" She glanced at her daughter and her face fell. "Except my mom won't be back to watch Emaline until this afternoon."

He scratched his jaw. "You can always bring her. If you want."

"You sure?"

He nodded. It wasn't like she was applying at some fancy big-city law firm or anything. They were a family-owned business, after all. He'd spent a good chunk of his childhood in his parents' office, from as early as he could remember. Besides, like his mom had said, they needed the help and Harper needed employment.

"Okay." She eyed her T-shirt and jeans. "Give me a minute to change." Smoothing a hand over her baby's head, she kissed her temple then dashed inside.

CJ meandered back to his truck and waited, leaning against the passenger side. When Harper reemerged, he hurried to carry her car seat and diaper bag. With one under his arm, the other draped over his shoulder, he opened her door for her.

"Thank you."

He nodded. He cast her a sideways glance, his chest aching at the memory of her expression the day she'd walked away. Eyes cold, chin raised. As if he'd meant nothing to her.

With Emaline secured in her car seat, he shifted into Drive, and he gave himself a mental shake. Rehashing the past would only stir up seeds of bitterness it'd taken years to kill.

After successfully avoiding interacting with CJ for nearly six months, not an easy task in a town Sage Creek's size, here she sat in his truck, for the second day in a row. Based on his stiff posture, he wasn't too thrilled with this arrangement, either.

She wouldn't blame him if he hated her. Yet, tense body language aside, he was going out of his way to help her.

That had always been his way.

He cast her a sideways glance. "Any chance you brought your car keys with you? I can tinker with your engine some this afternoon."

She nodded, dug through her diaper bag and handed them over. "Want my debit card? In case you need to buy parts?"

Staring through the windshield, he dragged the back of his hand under his jaw. Then he shook his head. "I can catch you on the back end, if need be."

She had a feeling he planned to cover whatever expenses arose. While she appreciated his generosity, she bristled at what felt like pity. The state of her bank account, and her love for Emaline, pushed her to swallow her pride. For now. She could revisit the conversation later. The air in his cab was thick enough.

He drummed his fingers on the steering wheel. "How are your parents? Your dad still driving semis?"

"Sort of, but for a moving company based in Houston."

Unfortunately, her father had never been one to stay at the same job for long, and his inconsistent employment history had finally caught up with him. If only her mom had finished her teaching degree when she'd had the chance, they wouldn't be in such a financial mess now. But she'd been so "head over heels in love" that she'd withdrawn to follow Harper's dad doing feed delivery to Sage Creek. The hourly pay had looked good in the classifieds, but not so much when bills had come due.

He'd spent the years since bouncing from one hiring bonus to the next.

Facing the rear, Emaline started to coo and kick her feet.

Amusement lit CJ's eyes. "Really, now?" He slipped his index finger into her fisted hand and gave a gentle tug. "Sounds like you're telling tales to me."

Harper thought back to the evenings when he used to hop the fence between his place and the children she babysat for's. It had never taken him long to pull the kids into a game, and always one in which he'd found some way to display his agility. She'd been flattered to think such a popular, good-looking upperclassman wanted to show off for her.

When they reached the hardware store, he dropped her and Emaline at the front entrance, parked, then met them inside.

He nodded to an older gentleman with a large protruding gut and crooked nose. Typing into his phone, CJ led her to the break room. She let her gaze linger over his carved statues as they passed that area once again, impressed by his talent. Had he always been this creative? If so, he'd never mentioned anything.

What else didn't she know about him?

"Have a seat." He motioned to the same table she'd sat at to fill out her application.

Palms sweaty, she chose the chair facing the door. The space smelled like a mixture of coffee, popcorn and pizza—an odd combination for ten in the morning. Then again, the Jenkinses probably started their day at dawn's first glow.

CJ strode to the counter lining the opposite

wall and opened the cupboard above the sink. "Can I get you a cup of coffee or some water?"

"I'm good, but thank you." Her daughter reached for her earrings.

Harper faced her outward and bounced her on her knee. What if CJ's mom wasn't as keen on her bringing Emaline with her as CJ had thought? Harper probably should've insisted they schedule the interview for another time, but he'd caught her off guard, showing up like he had. As had the phone call he'd received from his mom.

With the way Nancy had scowled at her twice—first when she'd come to apply then again at church—Harper had assumed the Jenkinses had slammed this door shut. Upon seeing it inch open, she knew she needed to jam her foot in before the woman changed her mind.

Footsteps approached moments before CJ's mom entered. "Thank you for coming in." Nancy's stiff smile softened slightly as her gaze pinged from Harper to her daughter making raspberry noises around the fist shoved into her mouth. "And this sugarplum is?"

"Emaline."

"Beautiful name for a beautiful girl." She caressed the baby's cheek with the back of her hand, glanced at CJ, then took the seat directly across from Harper.

He chose the one kitty-corner to them both. "I

told her she could bring the little one, this being so last minute and all."

"That's fine." She placed Harper's application on the table, backside up, and scanned her references. "I see you've been working at the library for going on six months now."

"Yes, ma'am."

"Seems a fitting employment. You always were quite the reader." She rested folded hands in front of her. "I must say, I am a bit surprised you'd want to work at a hardware store. We make a point to treat our employees well and pay a fair wage, but this isn't a cakewalk. You'll work up a sweat. Get your hands dirty. Might even break a nail."

Harper flinched inwardly at the sarcastic remark but did her best to keep her expression pleasant. "I'm prepared to work hard, ma'am."

"You'd be working under CJ. Would that be a problem?"

Her gaze shot to him, her face warm. "No, ma'am." She had to believe their interactions wouldn't always feel so strained and awkward. They were adults, after all.

Nancy asked a few more standard questions, such as the days and hours she could work, then indicated for her son to take over.

He shifted his chair closer. "I noticed on your résumé you worked with a traveling dance company. I know that was always your dream. Congrats."

She almost believed he meant that. "Thank you."

"Then, after, as a waitress in Seattle for a few months. Why'd you leave?"

She dropped her gaze before forcing herself to make eye contact. Her answer would only prove she hadn't achieved the success she'd so confidently predicted upon receiving her college acceptance letter. Not that he and the rest of Sage Creek hadn't figured that out already. She was living with her mom, working a part-time, minimum-wage job, after all.

Did that give him some level of satisfaction? A sense of vindication?

No. He'd never been the spiteful type. His gentle nature had surprised her, as had his down-to-earth personality, especially considering his muscular build and striking good looks.

Over half the girls at school had openly pined after him. She could still picture the chain reaction he'd initiated whenever he walked down the halls. Heavily hair-sprayed heads would turn, conversations growing more animated, high-pitched giggles following one after another like toppling dominoes.

Awaiting her answer, CJ rolled a pencil back and forth on the table.

She exhaled and wiped a sweaty palm on her leg. "Cost of living was high, and with my student loan payments, I just couldn't make ends meet."

He nodded. "Understandable. We're especially looking for someone with management potential."

The look his mom shot him suggested his statement surprised her.

He continued, "What do you see yourself doing five years from now?"

Another question to which she lacked a flattering answer. "Do I see myself in a leadership role, you mean? I suppose that's always a possibility." That was true enough, especially if she were able to become self-employed as a dance choreographer. But the twinge in her gut indicated her vagueness ventured on deception.

"Let me rephrase that for him." Nancy brought fisted hands beneath her chin. "If hired, how long do you anticipate staying on?"

If she told them the truth, they'd never hire her and, without this job, she'd never save enough to get out of Sage Creek. The epitome of an ironic catch-22. But neither could she lie to them. That didn't mean, however, that she needed to divulge everything. While she hated being so disingenuous, she wasn't just thinking about her dreams.

She needed to consider Emaline, too, and raising a child was expensive.

Harper squared her shoulders and kept her gaze leveled on Nancy. "I plan to be a hardworking, faithful employee focused on helping the store thrive."

Feeling the intensity of their eyes on her, she sensed her breathing shallow and quicken.

The ticking of the clock sounded loud in the tense silence that stretched between them.

Muted voices drifted toward them, then passed by.

Emaline started to fuss. With the baby leaning back against her stomach, Harper wiggled her thumbs in front of her, then jostled her arms once she clamped on. It didn't help.

This was far from a successful interview.

"I'll take the munchkin so you can focus." Nancy extended her hands.

Harper bit the inside of her cheek. "Are you sure?" Maybe holding a baby would soften Nancy's coarse demeanor, not that her obvious hostility was unreasonable.

"I've soothed an unhappy little one a time or two." Pushing back from the table, she took Emaline and rose. "Any other information we should know or that you'd like us to consider?"

Seemed Nancy had already made her decision,

and that it would not go in Harper's favor. "Just that I'm a quick learner and a hard worker."

CJ studied her. "This isn't agricultural science, obviously, and none of us expect you to stay on the rest of your life." The look his mom shot him suggested she felt differently. "But we don't want to waste employee hours, either, and training takes time."

"I know how to use the cash register."

Gently bouncing Emaline, Nancy scoffed. "Honey, we don't do that sort of specialization here. We're all-hands-on-deck. Expect everyone to pull their weight. Back to my question. If we hire and train you, how long are you planning on sticking around?"

"I really need this job." She forced the words out and fought the urge to break eye contact.

CJ observed her a moment longer. When he said nothing more, his mom returned Emaline. "Thank you for coming in." She walked to the door, clearly intending for Harper to do the same.

No "We'll get back to you"?

"Yes, ma'am."

Obviously, she did not get the job, which, her sad bank account aside, wasn't entirely terrible. At least now she and CJ could return to avoiding one another.

Chapter Four

CJ's mom watched Harper leave then turned back around. "That was a train wreck."

He shrugged. "I'm not too surprised. Now what?"

She raked her fingers through her hair. "You asking me what I want to do or what I think we should do?"

"The baby?"

She gave a one-shouldered shrug. "That and... well, we do need help."

"But what if we give her the job and she high-tails it out of town by summer's end?"

"Wouldn't be much different than hiring a high school student, except that she'd be spending her paycheck on diapers instead of junk food and whatnot."

He sighed. "I guess."

She looped an arm around his waist and gave

a squeeze. "You think you could handle having her around?"

He scoffed. "Of course."

She regarded him with a raised brow.

"Seriously. I'm over her."

Then why did he still feel that ache in his gut whenever she was around?

Memories of a painful season, nothing more.

Nancy's phone chimed and she glanced at the screen and frowned. "Your dad needs help in lumber with a disgruntled customer."

"Want me to come?" Why did he feel the need to insert himself into yet another encounter that would only set his nerves on edge?

"Nah." She waved a hand. "I'm sure it's nothing a smile and some extra attention can't fix. Most likely something's just gotten lost in translation." She hurried out to do one of the things she did best—make sure people knew they were more than dollar signs.

He poured himself a cup of coffee then paused, mug in hand, to scan his email inbox. Most of the messages were spam. The Williamses had sent out a request for childcare volunteers for their midweek recovery group meeting held at the church. A buddy's kid was selling overpriced candy bars to raise money for peewee soccer uniforms.

A subject line halfway down caught his attention. A woodworking club he'd joined a while back had forwarded information on an upcoming chain-saw carving festival held in San Angelo. Some called that city the art capital of Texas.

He opened the message and scanned the information. A live contest where people were given a set amount of time to create their best work. Winner receives five thousand dollars, a feature in a nationally known craftsman magazine, and all contestants would have the opportunity to sell their items on consignment.

He scrolled back to the top. They were hosting the event in two weeks. That wouldn't give him much time to practice. Too bad he couldn't submit something he'd already made. There were a bunch of his items gathering dust in the far corner of the store.

Still, it was worth a try. If he did well, he'd walk away with a chunk of change to put toward his buddy's building.

Hurried footsteps approached moments before Harper appeared in the open doorway. "I hate to be a pain, but I sort of need a ride home."

"Oh. Right. I parked in the back." He led her out to his truck and opened her door for her. "I'll go work on your vehicle after I drop you off."

"Want me to come?"

A jolt shot through him, clearly from emotional memory rather than anything related to how he felt now, because that was most certainly what he *didn't* want. If he had his choice, he'd spend as little time with her and her adorable baby as possible since, based on his gut reaction, every moment they spent together was sure to lead him down dangerous ground.

"Nope." He turned the ignition. "It could take a while."

She observed him with a furrowed brow, and he feared she might insist. But then she nodded. "If you're sure."

"Yep. I'll come get you when I'm done so you can drive it home."

"You think you'll be able to fix it today?"

"Should."

"Just let me know what it costs."

He wasn't sure how to respond, so he simply offered one quick noncommittal nod.

If she had money to spare, she never would've applied at the hardware store. But he also remembered how prideful she could be, especially when it came to money. He figured this stemmed from hanging out with the rich kids while growing up without funds for the latest clothing styles and other petty things the popular kids used to separate themselves from everyone else.

He veered onto a residential street beneath a canopy of intertwined tree branches. A gentle breeze stirred the leaves, causing splashes of light to dance on the asphalt. Ahead, two teenagers on skateboards, both wearing hoodies, zigged diagonally back and forth across the road. A runner passed from the opposite direction.

Her mom stepped outside as he pulled into her driveway, her toothy grin and energetic wave suggesting she'd sprung to false conclusions upon seeing Harper in his pickup. He'd barely shifted into Park before she was standing outside the passenger's-side door.

He stepped out and rounded the truck to help Harper with Emaline. "Ma'am." He tipped his hat at Harper's mom.

Patricia's wide grin revealed crooked, coffee-stained teeth. "CJ. So good to see you again."

He winced inwardly, knowing she attached too much meaning to his being at their place two days in a row. "You, too, ma'am." She had to know about Harper's application and broken-down vehicle. Although a person could still misread between the lines, making too much of something as simple as a kind gesture.

He carried the now-empty car seat to the stoop and set it to the right of the door.

Harper followed and placed her daughter in her mom's open arms.

Facing CJ, she lingered as the two went inside. "I really appreciate your help. With the car, taking the time to interview me." Her expression suggested his kindness had caught her off guard, and maybe even filled her with a twinge of remorse for how she'd ended things.

Now who was the one attaching deeper meaning to what was nothing more than a normal display of gratitude? And why? Because he wanted her to know how much she'd hurt him? That wouldn't change anything.

He hooked a thumb through his belt loop. "That's the Sage Creek way. We help one another when we've got the means." Had she missed that when she'd lived in Seattle?

Two boys barreled out of the adjacent house, hooping and hollering. A moment later, a pregnant woman with spiked black hair and combat boots emerged and sat on the top step. She was talking to someone on the phone.

Harper's mom reappeared without the baby.

Partially facing Harper and partially facing the street, CJ slid her a sideways glance. "Guess I best get."

"Girl, where are your manners?" Mrs. Moore crossed her arms. "Show the man some appreciation."

Harper's eyes widened and she stammered. "I don't get paid until—" She looked at her mom. "Do you have any money I can borrow until Friday?"

CJ raised his hands, palms out. "No need to pay me. Elbow grease is free."

And as to whatever parts he might need to buy, Pastor Roger often talked about how a person's checkbook tended to reflect their heart. Seemed if he couldn't help a single mom working part-time for minimum wage, he needed to rethink his convictions.

"Well, then, the least we can do is send you off with a full belly." Patricia Moore smiled.

"That's mighty kind of you, ma'am, but I've already had breakfast. Plus, I should really get moving on your daughter's car."

If his mom were here, she'd find his refusal of Southern hospitality rude. Then again, she might make exceptions, considering who'd made the offer.

"There's always room for a nice, fat piece of chocolate cake." She took his arm and tugged him inside.

"Mama!" Voice tight, Harper dashed in after them.

Patricia pulled CJ, stunned, into the kitchen, despite her daughter's protests. "Park yourself, sugar." She motioned to one of four mismatched chairs positioned around a slightly lopsided table covered with a blue-and-green plastic tablecloth. Frog-shaped salt and pepper shakers, a bottle of hot sauce and a small cactus with fuzz-like spikes centered the space.

"Go on, now." She gestured once again for him

to take a seat. "Otherwise, I'll think you don't like my baking."

If only he had a pressing meeting to attend, then he could provide a legitimate reason to leave. Without a polite reason to decline, he soon found himself sitting across from his ex-girlfriend, who suddenly appeared reluctant to meet his gaze. She'd placed Emaline at her feet in one of those bouncy contraptions with something resembling a colorful abacus forming two crisscrossing arches from one side of the doohickey to the other. The baby seemed fascinated with a plush sunshine sprouting from an empty food tray.

The room hadn't changed much in the five years since he'd sat in this kitchen. Fake ivy dulled by a layer of dust stretched across the tops of the cupboards, draping down at the dish-filled sink. Numerous business card magnets held a mass of pictures, pizza coupons and newspaper clippings to the fridge door, and two stained towels hung from the handle on the oven door. The room itself smelled like a mixture of vinegar, cinnamon and burned food.

"How're your folks doing?" Mrs. Moore sliced three pieces of cake, set them on saucers and distributed one to each of them. "Things picking up at the store, now that it's spring?"

"Yes, ma'am. A lot of folks are fixing to garden, take care of their lawn and whatnot. We also tend to see more of our contractors this time of year through the summer."

"So, you could use Harper's help." She shot her daughter a wink and dropped into an open chair. "My girl was a smidgeon nervous about applying, but I told her she had nothing to fret about. You've always done the hard right thing. I admire that about you, and I'm grateful that you've got my daughter's back. Everyone needs someone with influence in their corner, right?"

Her question felt like a veiled way to pressure CJ to leverage his relationship with his parents to play favorites—with a woman who wasn't exactly high on any of their most-esteemed list.

He searched his brain for the best way to answer. "We're thankful for the increased business."

Her mother scoffed. "You sound like a politician. But I get it. Can't exactly go talking—"

"Mom!" Cheeks flushed, Harper narrowed her eyes. She shifted her attention to CJ. "Do you still restore car engines?"

He shook his head. "Haven't done much of that since my old school buddy Crosby and I tinkered with the beast." That's what they'd called the 1950 peacock blue pickup his friend had purchased dirt cheap at a salvage lot. Their initial plans to fix it up and sell it to fund a camping trip had turned into a mutual hobby. "His parents got tired of having a messy garage and a couple of clumsy teenagers spilling oil all over the place."

"I remember how cluttered your workplace had been." Her strained chuckle suggested she didn't enjoy this forced gathering any more than he did. Yet Southern manners kept them both there, responding politely to her mother's conversation.

"Speaking of memories." Patricia gave one clap and sprang to her feet. "I'll be right back." She darted out and soon returned with a light pink photo album with a cover bordered by interloping flowers. "Do you remember when you first came over for supper?"

He swallowed. "A bit." What did the woman want? She hadn't been this talkative since the time she'd come into the store looking for free plumbing help if she bought the material.

She laid a hand on his arm. "Believe that was Harper's freshman year. That would've made you, what? A junior?"

"Yes, ma'am."

"He doesn't want to look at these." Based on Harper's strained expression, she felt even more uncomfortable than he did.

"Oh, hush now." Patricia waved a hand and refocused on CJ. "That evening, you were so nervous, you were visibly shaking."

He'd had no intention of coming then any more than he had today. Yet he'd found himself sink-ing into their sagging sofa, concerned her mom had no intention of letting him leave.

"Ah, here we are." Album on the table, she angled it so everyone could see the pictures taken at a makeshift photo booth set up by the local library. On one section of wall, they'd hung a background of heavily knotted wood paneling painted on butcher paper and had gathered several props—hats, comically large glasses, feather boas and various cutouts sold in party stores.

He and Harper had stayed long enough to put on nearly every item and probably used up way too much of the library's Polaroid film. In the end, they'd only kept three photos—the two in Mrs. Moore's album and another tossed in the trash a few months after Harper had ditched him to move to Seattle.

Forearm on the table, Harper leaned forward. "You saved that?" Her voice carried a note of nostalgia that clenched his jaw.

"Of course," Patricia said. "It was your first real date, after all. Before I'd given you permission to start dating, I might add."

Harper's laugh sounded strained. "Well, you hadn't said no, either. Just that you'd think about it."

Her mom scraped frosting off the top of her cake. "Which you took advantage of." She made eye contact with CJ. "Had a mind to toss you out."

That wasn't how CJ remembered things. Matter of fact, Mrs. Moore had been about as friendly as when she'd pulled him inside today.

"That was an expensive little outing." Harper quirked an eyebrow at CJ. "How much money did you spend on that coin toss game?"

He chuckled. "Considering I never did win the panda bear I promised you, at least ten dollars too many."

It was comical, looking back on it now, how competitive he'd become. Seemed whether on the football field or at a small-town carnival, his drive to win rose up—that and his desire to please Harper.

A goal that had ultimately ended in failure.

"But you did get me that big hand with the pointing finger."

"I redeemed myself then." Their jaunt down memory lane roused conflicting emotions within him. A latently bitter part of him he'd thought he'd overcome stirred him to end this conversation and leave. But there was also a tiny part of him that wanted to stay. To hear her laugh and drift back, even for a moment, to the time when he'd felt profoundly happy.

Only to feel as if someone had literally ripped his heart from his chest four years later.

He finished the last bite of his cake then pushed up from the table. "Thank you for your hospitality, ma'am."

Her mother sprang to her feet. "I'll see you out." She led the way to the door, Harper following. "Now, don't be a stranger, you hear?"

With a polite but noncommittal nod, he descended the steps, pausing when Harper called out to him.

"I really appreciate this."

The vulnerability in her eyes left him feeling off kilter. It evoked too many memories from their past when she'd sought strength in his embrace. "I'll text you once I know for sure what the problem is and about how long it'll take me to fix it."

"Do you have my number?"

"Not on me."

"Give me your cell and I'll add my contact info."

He hesitated, reluctant to create yet one more connection between them.

It felt like the invisible barriers they'd managed to maintain between them were crumbling. Worse, there was a small rebellious part of him that felt okay with that. A part of him that could easily hope for more, if he let himself.

That, he refused to do.

Harper returned to the kitchen to clean up their cake plates.

Her mom entered a few moments later, humming a familiar tune and carrying her basket of yarn and knitting needles. "That sure was a pleasant and unexpected little visit." She set her craft items on the table, next to the still-open photo album. "I take it your interview this morning went well?"

Harper frowned, thinking back to the expression on CJ's face when he'd asked about her long-term plans. It was almost as if he'd known she didn't intend to stay.

She was probably being paranoid.

"Not exactly." She relayed the discussion.

Her mom's brow creased. "Guess you best apply somewhere else."

"I know."

"Look, I don't want to tear down your rainbow or nothing, but it might be time to change directions. You've told me how competitive the dance industry is."

She regretted telling her mom that, but, at the time, she'd felt it necessary to explain why she'd needed to move back home. It had felt less like a failure. "I've never shied away from a challenge, and with hard work and perseverance—"

"As I told you before when you were hemming and hawing about applying at the hardware store, your circumstances have changed. You've got a baby to think of now."

Her mom's words picked at an old wound. Tears stung her eyes at the reminder of just how little her parents had truly believed in her. Growing up, while they'd never outright discouraged her from pursuing dance, neither had they offered much support.

She'd been the one to pay for her lessons and summer camps through babysitting, washing people's cars, tutoring younger students and whatever other means she could find. She'd even had to find and secure her own rides once she'd progressed beyond Sage Creek Dance Academy to a more advanced program in Houston. Thankfully, she'd learned about a girl taking weekend classes at one of the city's community colleges. She'd driven her to and from. She'd also allowed Harper, with permission from the family the girl rented a basement bedroom from, to crash on an air mattress in her room.

"I don't mean to sound harsh." Her mom's needles clicked and clacked. "And I know how it feels to change your plans and have to give something up. I just want you to be realistic, is all."

"By that you mean trading my dreams to spend the rest of my life working piecemeal minimum-wage jobs?" Her tone came out harsher than she'd expected.

"There are worse things."

She knew her mom spoke from experience. She'd gotten married the week after she'd finished her freshman year in college. Prior, she'd been struggling to work and go to school, and spending a bit too much time in extracurricular activities. Then she'd met Harper's dad, and the two had fallen hard for each other. When he'd learned about the feed driver job with a large hire-on bonus, he convinced her mom to drop out of school and move with him to Sage Creek, Texas.

From Harper's perspective, the rest of their story was far from happily-ever-after. Her dad was rarely around, money was always tight and, when he was around, her parents spent most of that time arguing. She suspected her mom harbored resentment for choosing his career over hers.

Harper wouldn't follow in her footsteps.

She kissed her mother on the cheek, breathing in her strawberry-scented shampoo. "I appreciate your concern, and I greatly appreciate you allowing me and Emaline to stay while I get my feet back under me."

Her mom set her knitting down. "About that. I wanted to talk to you about something." She repeated what Harper had overheard that morning, adding, "Starting next month."

"Okay."

"I hope you know, I'm doing this for your own good. This might even help you realize what you could've had, and maybe even still can, with CJ."

Her jaw went slack. "You're not seriously suggesting we get back together for financial reasons. You should know me better than that."

"Motherhood changes things. And I saw his expression when I flipped to that photo booth picture of the two of you—and the way he looked at you. I don't know what all happened between you both. Figured you must've bushwhacked him good, with how he and his mom acted once you left. Still, after what I've seen today—if given the chance, he'd take you back. No doubt in my mind."

Harper's heart gave a lurch. Sucking in her breath, she shook her head. "Even if that were true—which it absolutely isn't—did you not notice his reluctance to come in today, or his hurry to leave?"

Patricia flicked a hand. "That don't mean nothing. He's fixing your car, isn't he?"

"You're misreading his kindly nature. Pretty sure he's done the same for numerous other people in this town." Back in high school, he used to mow the lawn for an older couple who lived next door. "Regardless, he and I are not getting back together because I'm not staying in Sage Creek."

Nor would he ever leave. He'd always been content to live in this town—and work for his parents—for the rest of his life. While she didn't fault him for that, she wanted more. For herself and Emaline.

Chapter Five

Harper had just put Emaline down for a late-afternoon nap when CJ returned to let her know that he'd fixed her vehicle.

"Wow, that was fast." She grabbed her purse from the tall, wobbly accent table just inside the door. "How much do I owe you?"

"Nothing. Now a good time for me to take you to your car?"

"Sure. Just give me a sec to let my mom know where I'm going." She dashed into the kitchen, told her mom she was leaving, then hurried outside.

CJ stood waiting at his truck and opened the passenger's-side door as she approached.

"Thank you." She dipped beneath his arm, her senses all too aware of his closeness. Averting her gaze, she busied herself with settling into her seat. Once he slid in beside her and pulled away from the curb, she returned to the safer topic—

for her emotions, not her pocketbook—of reimbursement.

"It's all good. Really." His firm tone said drop the subject.

Considering she was still waiting to hear back on her job application, she didn't want to do or say anything to potentially hinder his sense of good will. Yet letting the issue drop felt rude. But she also worried, should she push the matter further, it'd come off as nagging, and maybe even stubborn. Men in the South were trained in chivalry from the time they could string a sentence together—in Sage Creek especially.

He cast her a sideways glance. "Tell me more about your time dancing with that organization from Seattle. You do much traveling?"

"I did."

"Ever out of the country?"

She shook her head. "I wasn't that good."

"But you could've been, right?"

"That was my goal." Although she hadn't given up on that dream entirely, now that she had Emaline, she understood that she'd need to compromise. She wasn't an Anca Cojocaru or Céline Dupont, two of the highest paid dancers in the industry. No amount of frugal living would allow her to pay for a sitter to accompany her on tour.

However, she fully intended to earn enough to cover local daycare and cost of living. If only that wasn't increasing in nearly every city throughout the United States. Seattle especially. Yet others made it work.

He stopped at a four-way intersection. "What was your favorite place to visit?"

She angled her head, thinking back on what felt like a whirlwind career, however short. "Probably Denver. They've got great restaurants, museums, shopping districts with fun, independent boutiques, some 850 miles of paved bike trails. You can enjoy all the benefits of the city while living within thirty minutes of incredibly beautiful hiking."

A frown flashed across his face before smoothing into his previous casual expression. "Sounds like a fun place to visit. Did you get to do much exploring?"

"Sometimes, especially when we stayed in one location for a few weeks."

"That must've been quite the adventure. I imagine that felt good, to achieve something you worked so hard for."

Focusing on her hands, Harper gave a slight nod. The experience had changed and matured her. She'd loved every moment she'd danced on-stage, the preshow rehearsals, the bright lights, and the sound of applause that swirled throughout the auditorium. But her time with the company had also been tough. Hours spent on the bus, checking in and out of hotels, the increased intensity in the rehearsals. Mostly, however, she'd felt lonely—like the annoying little sister who was always hanging around, hoping she'd be included.

The competitive, cutthroat culture that had permeated the organization had left her feeling unsettled and insecure. She'd been so desperate for a friend. That was probably why she'd been so blinded by the charm displayed by Emaline's father.

"You okay?" CJ studied her with a furrowed brow.

She forced a smile. "Yeah. Just thinking."

"About?"

She took a breath and gave herself a mental shake. "Finishing our conversation regarding how I can reimburse you for your time and money spent fixing my car."

"I already told you—"

"I'm not a charity case, CJ." Although, she didn't exactly have money to spare, a fact her application had probably broadcasted. But neither was she a leech, which is how his random acts of kindness were beginning to make her feel. "If you won't let me pay you back financially, at least let me return the favor in some way."

He quirked an eyebrow and turned into the church parking lot. "What're you thinking?"

Great question. "Do you need any yard work done?"

His lips inched toward a smile. "You do land-scaping now?"

She picked at a hangnail. "No, but I can mow."

"Four acres?"

She swallowed. "How much is that?"

"Three football fields."

"Oh." She studied him. "Your yard is seriously that big?"

"My property, yeah—the cleared portion. With trees, it's just shy of six. Horse pasture takes up two of those acres."

She released a breath. "Okay. So that leaves… what?" She calculated the number in her head and frowned. "An acre. Your lawn's that big?"

"Uphill both ways."

She laughed. "You're messing with me."

He shrugged. "Some. My yard truly is a full acre. A bit more, actually, and behind the house, it is pretty hilly. But I don't need any help with it. I purchased a riding lawn mower for super cheap a few years back. One of the perks of working in a hardware store."

She rubbed the back of her arm, trying to think of another option. "I could make you dinner."

He seemed surprised. "Since when did you learn to cook? Because I distinctly remember you burning instant mashed potatoes."

She laughed, thinking back to the time she'd

tried to cook him a meal. "I've grown up a bit since my high school days."

"And learned to boil water?"

"Quit being a stink."

He raised a hand, palm out. "Hey, if you want to throw a couple chicken breasts on the stove, I'm game."

A couple? Did that mean he expected them to eat together? Would it seem odd for her to leave without doing so?

Regardless, she'd promised something she didn't have the skills to deliver, as much as she wished otherwise. She highly doubted boxed macaroni and bagged salad would constitute a fair exchange.

She released a breath. "Maybe me in the kitchen isn't such a great idea, unless you point me to a sink full of dishes." She brightened. "Housework!" She snapped her fingers. "I bet you don't like scrubbing floors and bathrooms."

The skin crinkled around his eyes. "Can't say that's my favorite way to spend an off day."

"Perfect. I'll come clean your place then." She was off the next day, as was her mom, which meant she could tend to Emaline. "How about tomorrow?"

Stopping beside her compact, he cut the engine. Someone driving by on the adjacent street honked. The wind blew a garbage sack across the asphalt. The afternoon sun dimmed behind drifting clouds, then brightened again.

She huffed. "Come on, CJ. Don't be so stubborn. Actually, *elitist* is a better word."

He scoffed. "What?"

"You can give it out but can't take it. Seriously, how would you respond if our roles were switched?"

"I'd be worried about my car."

She rolled her eyes. "You know what I mean. If I were the one helping you out with something like this."

"That's different."

"Why? Because I'm a woman or because I have a kid? What makes me inherently inferior?"

He opened his mouth then closed it. He swiped a hand over his face. "I get it. You're right."

She reached for her purse, stopped and fell against her seat back. "Look, I'm broke, okay, which you obviously assumed." *Way to fight for something only to backpedal once you got it.* Regardless, she would not lose her sense of human dignity to someone with a hero complex. "But I'm not helpless, nor do I want your handout." Her eyes stung. Blinking, she turned and reached for the door handle before he could see her building tears.

"I'm sorry. I was acting like a clueless jerk." He placed a gentle hand on her shoulder. "I would love for you to come and clean my house. Although you should know, it's a mite messy."

She grinned. "Perfect. When would you like me to stop by?"

He drummed his fingers on the steering wheel. "I'm off most any night this week—after six or so."

"I mostly work afternoons, but I'm off tomorrow. Is that too soon?"

"That'll work. I'll text you my address."

Wait a minute. Had she really just invited herself to his house? Now that their plans were set, the notion of her spending time in his home, with him there, felt much too intimate.

The next afternoon, CJ put misplaced plumbing parts in the right places, educated a woman on what tools to buy to retile her bathroom and made some calls to schedule upcoming deliveries. Then, after a quick visit to the storage area to ensure all their shipments had gone out for the day, he looked for his mom to let her know he was leaving.

He found her in electrical, working through an inventory sheet attached to a clipboard. She turned to him with a warm smile. "You finished for the day?"

"Yep." He relayed what he'd done and what he'd communicated with Ken, a retired schoolteacher who worked for his parents.

She studied him with a furrowed brow. "You in a hurry?"

Her expression suggested she was concerned about something. "Not hugely." He could always shoot Harper a text saying he'd be late, if need be. "What's up?"

"Your father and I have decided to hire Harper. We know, based on past experience, this could come back to bite us. But we're trusting that she's grown up since her high school days. If not... well, I guess that's a risk we're willing to take." She exhaled. "Back when y'all were kids, I told her I loved her like a daughter."

"I remember." Along with every word he'd ever told Harper, as well, and all the promises she'd made in return.

"This morning, as I read my Bible about the kind of love we receive from Christ, I sensed Him asking me to show that same love to Harper. The kind that reaches out, even when a person isn't acting all that loveable. Because that's what God has called us to do."

"Okay." He hated to admit it, but he agreed. As challenging as it would be working alongside Harper each day, his mom had always raised him to do the hard right thing.

She took his hand in hers. "But I don't want to hurt you, or make this a miserable place for you to work."

"I'm good. I promise."

She gave one quick nod. "I'll call her in the morning."

CJ shifted. "I can tell her. I'll see her tonight, anyway."

Her lips flattened into a firm line. "What do you mean?"

He explained their arrangement. "I understood where she was coming from."

"I'm worried that you might be finding reasons, subconsciously, to spend more time with her."

He snorted. "What? Of course not. I'm simply trying to help a single mom who appears to be down on her luck."

His mother studied him. "Be careful, CJ."

"Not sure what danger there could be in pushing a vacuum around, but okay."

"You know what I mean."

"If you're worried about me falling for her again, I can assure you that won't happen. I'm not that foolish. Experience taught me she'll bail as soon as something more exciting comes along."

"You may be right. Just make sure she doesn't take a piece of your heart with her."

"Hardly." He kissed her cheek. "Seriously. You've got nothing to fret about."

"But I'm a mom. Pretty sure worrying is part of my job description." She glanced past him toward the end of the aisle. "That, and figuring out where all of our fifty-two-inch distressed wood ceiling fans went, because my records show we should have fifteen, but I only see eleven on the shelves."

"A lot of those boxes do look alike. Someone probably got in a hurry and put a bunch of them in the wrong place. Want me to stick around to sort them all out?"

"No. You've been here long enough, especially with it being your off day and all."

CJ hadn't had much of those since they'd lost Albert, an older farmer who'd worked part-time to supplement his income. A few months ago, he'd decided to sell it all and move to Florida, near his daughter, son-in-law and grandkids. Since he'd left at the beginning of winter, when sales were beginning to dip, Nuts, Bolts and Boards had managed well.

When spring hit and folks started coming out of figurative hibernation, however, they'd realized just how shorthanded they were. With Albert's work ethic and over ten years of store experience, they'd about need to hire two people to take his place.

The more Harper worked, the less CJ would need to. Then maybe he could cut his hours here and devote more time to his carvings.

"See you in the morning." He let his mom give him a sideways squeeze then strolled to the back of the store, through the lumber and to his truck sitting near their overflowing dumpster.

Once behind the wheel, he shot Harper a text to let her know he was heading home, along with a You can still back out.

She responded with an almost immediate Nice try. Leaving soon.

She arrived at his place moments after him and parked alongside the storage shed where he kept all his tools. She seemed to hesitate, almost as if fortifying herself, before stepping out of her vehicle.

He found himself doing the same thing, though perhaps for different reasons. Even in her gym shorts and an old softball jersey, her hair pulled back in one of those messy buns, she looked beautiful. Her erect posture, toned legs and over-all fit frame testified to her years of dancing. The early evening sun glimmered on her glossy pink lips and highlighted the mahogany streaks in her hair.

She gazed across the land. "It's so beautiful out here."

He tried to view his property through her eyes. Directly in front of them, an old maroon barn centered a section of pasture with taller grass dotted with purple, yellow and red flowers. Beyond that, clouds drifted above gently sloping hills hemmed in by a grove of trees on either side.

His house itself, a single-story painted white with sage trim, wasn't much to look at. He'd built the simple covered porch and had added lattice beneath it, placing limestone and sandstone boulders surrounded by river rocks. He'd also carved the three Texas stars decorating the gable.

Harper rotated toward the corral and two-stall stable and gasped. "You have horses?"

"I do. A Morgan and quarter horse, both in their early teens and adopted from the horse rescue."

"That's awesome." Her gaze turned wistful. "I miss riding. I didn't do a whole lot of it as a kid. Only chance I got, really, was when I spent the night with Abigail. Her parents own a hobby farm close to the Owen place."

"I remember." He rubbed the back of his neck, feeling a nudge to invite her back to come riding. Seemed the kind thing to do.

He thought of his mom's statement prior to his leaving the store. *You might be finding reasons... to spend more time with her.*

While that was far from true, he agreed with the implication beneath her words. He and Harper would already be spending way too much time together without him adding cause for more.

"Well." Hands on her hips, Harper faced her car. "Guess I best get busy." She strode to her trunk. From it, she produced a large overstuffed tote with a fat roll of paper towels poking out the top.

"What's all this?" He led the way up his steps, the wooden boards sagging beneath them.

"I wasn't sure what all you had in terms of cleaning supplies."

Holding open the door, he motioned for her to enter. "In case I'm the stereotypical bachelor slob?"

She laughed. "I didn't say that." She stepped inside and made a visual sweep of the interior. Light streamed through the blinds, casting horizontal lines across the wooden floor. On the coffee table, made from a slab of wood with retained live edges, sat a pile of unopened mail, coasters formed from branch slices and a hobbit house carved from cottonwood bark.

She eyed some sketches he'd made in preparation for the chain-saw carving contest. "What are these? Do you mind?"

"Go ahead."

She picked up the pages, moving to the event details he'd printed from online. "You doing this?"

He shrugged and told her what he'd learned and his tentative plans. "Not sure how I'll do as I've never created anything with a timer ticking." He could easily spend months on a project, envisioning the final piece then allowing that image to change and evolve with every cut. "But figured there's no harm in trying."

"I'm sure you'll do great." She set the papers down. "You're super talented."

"Thanks."

It felt good to hear her affirmation and to know, based on the admiration in her eyes, that she meant it. Helped lessen the sting her words had left when he'd learned what she'd said about his lack of ambition. Maybe if she'd said that to him personally, in the heat of an argument or something, it wouldn't have cut so deeply. But the accusation had trickled back to him from one of her friends, which meant she'd been complaining about him, and thinking of leaving, while he'd thought all was good between them.

"Back to your slobby bachelor statement." Lips twitching toward a smile, she shot him a pointed look. "I did block off a full two hours for this endeavor."

"Ouch. Hopefully, it won't take that long." He wasn't exactly a neat freak, but he wasn't a careless frat boy, either.

She gave a simple shrug. "It's not like I have a jam-packed schedule or anything. I have quite a bit of extra time on my hands, actually." Her voice conveyed a trace of discouragement.

"Speaking of…my folks decided to give you the job."

Her face brightened. "Really? That's fantastic." Her enthusiasm revealed how much she needed additional work.

"When can you start?"

"Now?" Humor danced in her eyes.

"What? And leave me with a sink full of dirty dishes?"

"You're right. That would be heartless. Tomorrow?"

"That works." Their easy banter reminded him of the fun they used to have together. Back then, her simple presence had always added color to an otherwise dreary day. "How does 8:00 a.m. sound?"

"I'll need to make sure my mom can watch Emaline, but yeah. I should be able to do that."

She ran her hand across an oak chair with a curved seat and two-tone twisted legs, her gaze sweeping from it to his other furniture pieces positioned around the room. "Did you carve all this?"

The note of amazement in her voice made him stand taller. "I did."

"It's all so beautiful, although..." She frowned. "I have to admit, I was expecting more of a mess."

"You sound disappointed." Between working on his carvings, tending to his horses and the extra hours he'd been spending at the store, he hadn't had a lot of time to make much of a mess.

She shrugged and deposited her bag along the

wall next to the accent table formed from cedar roots. "Just want to make sure I'm actually being helpful, is all."

"You haven't seen the kitchen or bathroom."

"Should I be nervous?"

He chuckled. "Terrified."

"Challenge accepted." The way her smile brightened her eyes only added to her beauty, threatening to undo his resolve to maintain a safe emotional distance.

He cleared his throat. "Need anything from me?"

She glanced around. "Not that I can think of."

"All right." He backed toward the still-open door, increasing the distance between them. "I'll be outside."

"Okay. Thanks, CJ. Really. This might not seem like a big deal to you, letting me scrub your floors and all. But it means a lot to me." Her eyes carried a hint of vulnerability he found unnerving.

"No problem."

Stepping onto the porch, he took in a deep breath. That simple conversation should not have caused his pulse to increase the way it had.

His mom's warning was feeling more justified by the minute.

Chapter Six

The next morning, Harper arrived at Nuts, Bolts and Boards fifteen minutes early dressed in jeans and a navy V-necked T-shirt Trisha had said made her eyes pop. Wearing the earrings that always helped increase her confidence, she'd pulled her hair back in a loose ponytail. A few tendrils had slipped out and tickled her neck.

An older man with a white-and-brown-streaked beard and thinning hair approached. "Can I help you find something, ma'am?" The name tag attached to his coarse gray vest displayed the store name and logo.

She donned a wide smile and, initiating a handshake, introduced herself.

He nodded and brought a walkie-talkie from his belt to his mouth. "Got a gal here ready to work. Says her name's Harper."

The walkie crackled, then Nancy's voice followed. "Take her to the break room to clock in. CJ will be there shortly."

"Yes, ma'am." He returned the device to his belt and, with a tilt of his head, motioned for her to follow him.

Harper nodded and complied, breathing deep to calm her first-day jitters as they marched down the paint aisle, past CJ's amazing carvings and to where, she'd felt only days before, she had completely blown any chance of getting hired.

The man ambled to a metal time card cabinet attached to the far wall. "I'm Ken Palensky. I work Wednesdays, Fridays and Saturdays, 6:00 a.m. to 2:00 p.m." He pulled out one of the cards and a permanent marker from his vest pocket and handed her both. "Just add your name. Mr. or Mrs. Jenkins will fill in the rest."

"Okay, thank you."

Once done, she sat at the table to wait for CJ. He strolled in a moment later, cheeks slightly flushed, likely from some sort of strenuous activity on the store floor.

He offered a stiff smile. "Hey. Sorry to keep you waiting." He was dressed in his signature cowboy hat, sprinkled with a layer of sawdust, and appeared out of breath.

Because he'd hurried to see her? The thought sent a rush of warmth through her, doused by the reality check that followed. If he had hurried to the break room, that was only out of a supervisor-to-employee type of respect, and nothing more.

Besides, their relationship had ended years ago, and she had no intention of rekindling it.

Harper stood. "I haven't been here long." She handed him her time card, and he glanced at the clock on the machine.

"When did you get here?"

"Seven fifty," Ken answered for her.

CJ gave one quick nod. "Early. I like it."

Did she seem too eager? Then again, she was. She was broke, nearly out of gas, and Emaline was quickly outgrowing all of her clothes. Her desperate state sent a wave of shyness washing over her.

"We'll start you with the exciting stuff." Mirth lit his eyes. "Reading our training material."

"That's my cue to leave." Ken chuckled, then faced Harper. "Good to meet you, and welcome to the Nuts, Bolts and Boards family."

"Thank you."

Upon CJ's direction, she sat at the table and waited while he dashed out. He returned with a stack of papers stapled together, which he deposited in front of her. Typed in bold letters, the words "Volunteer Handbook and Safety Manual" dominated the front page.

He glanced at the clock on the wall above her. "I'll be back about eight thirty."

She nodded and settled in to read what she expected would be the most boring content since high school biology class. Her immediate goal? Finish without falling asleep. The fact that Emaline had woken her three times during the previous night would make that challenging.

Harper scanned the first page with a yawn. She could already feel her focus waning. Hopefully, there wouldn't be a test over this material. Midway through the second page, her eyelids began to droop. She sat back, shook out her arms, slapped her cheeks, then started again. She'd repeated the cycle three times and was contemplating splashing cold water on her face when CJ returned.

He stood beside her. "What'd I tell you? Fascinating stuff, right?"

His nearness sent a wave of heat through her. "Absolutely enthralling. What's next?"

"I'll give you a tour of the store. After that, you'll shadow me."

She'd assumed that would be the case when his mom had said she'd be working under him. But hearing him say it now caused her stomach to flutter in much the same way as it had back when they'd been dating.

Not a good sign.

Seattle. Dance choreographer and coach. She needed to focus on her dreams, of which working at a hardware store in Sage Creek, Texas, was not. If she wanted to be a teacher or hairdresser, or even barrel racing queen, maybe. But the one studio in the entire county only had classes through fifth grade. That meant there wasn't enough business to support her doing what she loved. If the studio owner decided to sell, maybe, but Harper wouldn't detour for a maybe.

CJ's voice cut through her thoughts. "For now, just give me, Ken or my parents a holler, and we'll get down whatever you need."

She followed his line of sight to the display of doors and trim lining the back wall. "What?"

"Just until we can get you forklift certified."

She nodded, as if his statement made perfect sense and she hadn't been completely zoned out. She really needed to catch up on her sleep soon, especially if he planned to train her to use some sort of powered apparatus to retrieve heavy items from uncomfortably high places. Were she to drop or break something, they'd fire her for sure. Maybe even take the breakage from her pay. Could they do that?

After a tour of the store, including of the lumber and customer pickup areas in the back, she shadowed CJ while he dealt with local contractors. A younger couple came in next, asking questions about tiling a bathroom. As CJ explained the process along with the tools they'd need to complete the project, Harper could see their enthusiasm fizzle. She wasn't surprised when they left without buying anything other than a gardening magazine displayed near the register.

Things remained slow but steady all day, although not busy enough for Mr. and Mrs. Jenkins to need additional help. Matter of fact, Harper couldn't remember when she'd ever seen more than a few customers in the store at a time. Then again, the Jenkinses were getting older. They hadn't had CJ until their forties. That put them in their sixties or so. Regardless, she hoped they wouldn't change their mind about hiring her. At least, not until she'd earned at least two months' worth of living expenses—a cushion to allow her to work toward her career goals.

If they gave her enough hours and she managed her money well, she could return to Seattle by summer's end, if not sooner. At least, that was the plan.

"Hey, CJ." They turned to see Ken approaching. "Got a gal asking questions about your carvings."

"Really?" His tone sounded hopeful. He glanced past him, then to Harper. "You mind?"

"Not at all. I'd enjoy hearing more about your work."

He studied her for a moment, his expression hovering between distrust and…appreciation?

Then he turned and headed in the direction from which they'd come.

At CJ's nook, or department, or whatever he called it, a short woman stood waiting next to a carving of a mother bear with two cubs crawling across a log behind her.

"Ma'am." CJ tipped his hat. "How can I help you?"

She had wiry gray hair, large orange earrings and wine-toned lipstick that bled into the fine lines around her mouth. "Are you the genius behind all of these wonderful pieces?"

He seemed to struggle for words. "More like a fella with too much time on his hands, but these are mine, yes."

The slight color to his cheeks suggested he wasn't any more comfortable receiving praise now than he had been back in high school. His humility had been one of the first things she'd noticed—an almost shocking characteristic for such a talented athlete.

"They are simply fabulous." The woman rotated, making a visual sweep of the space. "My granddaddy was a carver. Small stuff. Santas, ornaments, that sort of thing. Of course, never for money. Mostly made gifts for people.

"When did you start selling your items?"

CJ slid a hand into his pocket. "A few years ago."

"Really? How long has your work been displayed here?"

"About since I started."

She frowned and angled her head. "You serious?"

He nodded, looking confused.

"Sure wish I'd known. I would've purchased something for my son. He recently retired from the military, and he and his wife purchased the most adorable little cabin out on the lake in Tool. Would've loved to buy him that carving of that Sasquatch peeking around that tree trunk." She pointed. "He and the kids had a game they used to play when they went camping. Not sure how it started, but they'd grab binoculars and go searching for the big, hairy beast, as he called it."

Harper raised her eyebrows. "That didn't scare them?"

"Nah." The woman flicked a hand. "My son made the creature sound harmless. Said he lurked in the bushes, hoping to steal their chocolate bars."

CJ laughed. "Sounds like a fun dad. Tool's what? Three hours from here?"

"Thereabouts."

"If you still want to buy it, I could drive it to him for a reasonable delivery fee."

"Don't I wish. Unfortunately, we already busted the bank on his gift. But I'll certainly keep you in mind for the next time one of my men celebrate a major life event and I want to buy them something unexpected. You do special orders, if I want something particular?"

"Sure."

"I'll be back."

His posture slumped slightly. "Sounds good."

Harper watched the woman leave then turned to CJ. "That must have been encouraging."

"How so?"

"To have someone express such appreciation for your stuff."

"People can say a lot of things when their checkbooks aren't involved."

"You look disappointed."

"A bit surprised, maybe. That woman wasn't our most frequent customer, but she'd been in here enough that I would've expected her to have seen my work by now."

"I guess that just goes to show how people tend to have tunnel vision."

"And that I need to do a better job of promoting my carvings. Hopefully, the chain-saw contest will help with that. Assuming I do well enough to generate a buzz."

"Might not be that hard in a town the size of Sage Creek." She smiled. "People love to support their own."

He looked at her a moment, a teasing glint

in his eyes. "You saying that's the only reason I'll get people talking? That I'll fall flat on my face?"

"What? No, of course not. You'll do great. You're obviously super talented, to create all this." She made a wide sweeping motion with her arm. "You're very talented."

"Thank you." Still eyeing the Sasquatch, he scratched his jaw. "Although, I'd be happy just to make it into the Final Cut." He explained how almost anyone could participate as an amateur. "Artists competing in the televised portion, the only category with money attached, need a personal invite from the judges."

"How do you get that?"

"You send in a portfolio, which I need to work on, and footage in action. I don't expect to win. Not by a long shot. But that kind of exposure could launch me as an artist."

"I can help."

He stared at her a moment. "With what?"

"All of it." She grinned. "Taking pictures of your work, videotaping while you carve the stump. I can help you stretch your creativity muscles, too. I can share some tips designed to increase your divergent thinking skills."

"My what?"

"Basically, your ability to dream up innovative ideas."

"I see." His amused expression suggested he didn't find her suggestion all that plausible.

"Seriously. I can send you articles to back this up, but scientists call it neuroplasticity, which essentially refers to how our brain is constantly changing and adapting. Just give it a try. The way I figure it, you don't have anything to lose."

"Except time."

In other words, he viewed an afternoon or evening spent with her, outside of work, a loss. She'd been fooling herself to think he'd feel otherwise. Yes, he'd showed her kindness at the church event, in fixing her car, in helping her get this job and in patiently training her. But he'd clearly drawn the line when it came to stepping into this area of his life—the space where dreams live.

Looking away, she clicked her pinkie and thumb nails together. "It was just an idea."

"I appreciate it. I really do." Slipping a hand in his pocket, he studied her. "You know what? I'll try it." He paused. "So long as you don't ask me to do anything too goofy."

She laughed. "No promises."

"Oh, man. What have I gotten myself into?"

She could ask herself the same question because the more time they spent together, the more her heart threatened to tumble back into the old emotions that could've easily doused her dreams, had she let them.

But she hadn't, nor would she now, no matter how charming and handsome he could be.

What am I doing? A smart man would've declined Harper's invitation, and he still could. He could give her a reason why she couldn't help him after all, except that he did need her help.

Right?

His mom was too busy and leaned more to the logical, analytical side. He didn't want to bother his buddies Noah and Drake, although, if asked, they'd probably do about anything for him, taking random pictures and video recordings included.

He was way overthinking things.

With a mental shake, he refocused on his present responsibilities—familiarizing Harper with Nuts, Bolts and Boards.

"As you can see—" he motioned toward the shelves and the end of the aisle beyond "—we have numerous products. It'll take time for you to learn where everything is, but one of the best ways to do that is to work on returns. This is part of your job description anyway."

He led the way past the shelves with trim, doors and stairs to the customer returns area. Numerous items, from two-by-fours to lamps and tools, filled the large bins positioned behind a long, cluttered Formica counter. All the material clogging the small space was proof of their need for Harper.

Harper eyed a container of tools supporting a stack of lattice. "Do people ever buy something, use it, then bring it back for a refund?"

He followed her line of sight to a Spackle with a drop of paint on the handle. "Unfortunately, yeah. That happens quite a bit."

"Can you still resell them?"

"Unless it's broken or defective in some way. We just repackage it and put it back on the shelves." He picked up a gallon of paint in one hand and wood sealant in the other. "Saves time and steps to gather stuff stored in the same basic location. Grab that flat cart, will you?"

She complied and helped him stack primer, sealant, brushes, rollers and trays onto the cart. "Remember when you helped me paint my room?"

He chuckled. "Aqua and rose with a big ol' purple stripe? That I spilled on your carpet? Yeah." He'd knocked the entire can over, creating a puddle her cat had stepped in as they'd scrambled to clean up what they could. Thankfully, Harper had picked the cat up and placed him outside before he'd reached the hallway—but not before he'd left a trail of paw prints from the splotch to about a few feet from the door.

"I can still picture my mom's face when she

saw it. I thought she was about to have a heart attack."

"And I remember yours when she told you that you were going to have to replace the carpet."

"I don't know what I would've done if your parents hadn't sold me the materials at cost. And if you and your dad hadn't done the tearing up and laying down free of charge."

"Well, it was my fault." At the time, he'd been frustrated his folks hadn't comped the entire cost, or let him cover it all himself. But they'd felt strongly that both he and Harper needed to take responsibility for their mistakes. Now he understood and respected their decision.

She smiled. "The blame was mutual. And the situation wasn't a total loss. I did end up with new carpet, after all, which was much better than the stained and sun-bleached maroon I'd had before."

"Guess that's one way to get a remodel."

Cart loaded, he rolled it toward the paint aisle.

Someone called out to him as he passed the cash register. He turned to see a middle-aged woman approaching with a glossy book in one hand and a large quilted tote draped over her shoulder. She had shoulder-length blond hair and bangs that reached just below penciled-on eyebrows.

He recognized her from church, although he couldn't remember her name. "Yes, ma'am."

"My grandson will be staying with me over

spring break. He's ten and gets bored playing cards or dominoes or whatnot. I don't want him watching televisions or playing video games all the time, although he'd probably love that." She laughed. "I found this at a garage sale." She held up her book. "I thought maybe he and I could make something together, only I'm not sure what project would be best, with his age and all."

"Let's see what you've got." He glanced over her shoulder as she began turning pages, then looked at Harper. Her shift would be ending soon. "Can you give me one moment?"

"Of course."

He turned to Harper. "Do you think you can find where these go?" He motioned to the items in the cart.

She gave a slight laugh. "Eventually."

"You can clock out when you're done. See you at eight tomorrow? To shadow me again?"

Her smile was dangerously captivating him. "Sounds great."

He focused on the customer once again. "I love your desire to connect with your grandson. What a wonderful way to build lasting memories."

"I hope so. He is such a lovely child, and so imaginative. He spends hours building this three-dimensional virtual world, with detailed oceans, forests, bridges and castles. Of course, all while focused on a screen of some sort." She shook her

head. "He's asked me to join him, but it feels so...
I don't know. I guess this just shows that we're
from completely different generations. I want
to tap into some of that creativity—without the
need for a remote control." She smiled. "Then I
found this." She raised the book.

"It has some great options." He once again
scanned each project as she resumed turning
pages, and then tapped one of the diagrams.
"That boat wouldn't be too difficult. Then, after
the two of you build it, you could take him to the
lake to see if it floats."

"What a wonderful idea. We could make a day
of it. I could bring some kites and pack a picnic with strawberries and cookies. I always bake
batches of oatmeal raisin whenever he comes."

"That sounds delicious."

"Do you have a sweet tooth?"

He chuckled. "A bit."

"Well, then, I'll bring you some one of these
days."

"Oh, no. You don't have to do that."

"I want to." She patted his arm. "Consider it
my way of expressing my gratitude." She raised
an eyebrow. "You will help me find everything
I need, won't you?"

"Absolutely. Let's go get you some wood."

"I'll need tools, too. I'm not sure I even own
a screwdriver."

Oh, boy. Maybe the boat project wasn't the best idea. "Have you seen any of our kits?"

"I didn't know you carried such a thing."

"I'll show you."

Numerous questions and short stories later—of her grandson and his father when he was the same age—she selected a monster truck kit and a one-by-eight board for him to roll it down. CJ checked her out then headed to the office to gather his things.

His mom and Ken were talking just outside the break room. Based on the man's tense expression, it was about something unpleasant.

CJ stopped at their side. "Everything okay?"

Ken started popping his knuckles like he often did when nervous. "I messed up."

"How so?" Hopefully, he hadn't ordered something incorrectly for one of their contractors. Those guys often worked on a tight schedule.

"Crystal Simpson stopped in today, saw you training Harper and asked when y'all hired her on."

"Okay?" He looked between him and his mom. Had Harper done something concerning?

Ken squeezed the bill of his ball cap. "Wanted to know why no one called her son in for an interview."

CJ frowned. "Gael?" That guy would've been a great asset. Strong, hardworking, personable and, as far as CJ could tell, a person with integrity. "He was wanting to work here?"

Ken nodded. "He came in a couple of weeks ago. I was busy dealing with an upset customer, making a key for another gal, the phone was ringing and someone else was waiting for me to mix paint. You and your mama were off that morning, and your daddy was helping a builder in lumber. With all that going on, guess I didn't pay much attention when Gael handed me his application. I just set it with some other papers, my clipboard on top of it, then forgot all about it."

CJ released a breath and nodded. "Stuff happens."

The crevice between Ken's brows deepened. "I feel like I cost him his job. One, according to his mama, that he really needed. She didn't give specifics, but I got the sense the kid's in a bad place financially."

He placed a hand on Ken's shoulder. "I appreciate your compassion." The man had a big heart. "But there's not much we can do about that now." Although, they could bring the guy on, once CJ started devoting more time to his chainsaw carvings. Once his art earned the funds to allow for that.

Ken's hardened expression suggested he didn't much care for CJ's response. "Then I'll let you explain to Crystal, and her son, if he comes in asking, why we've got a ballerina working here rather than a fit young man with years of construction experience."

He stomped off before CJ could respond.

He turned to his mom. "Now what?"

She shrugged. "Do our best to soothe tempers?"

And if Ken, a man with an underdeveloped filter, drove Harper away?

CJ should find that prospect encouraging. Instead, it left a hollow feeling in his gut.

Chapter Seven

The next morning, Harper spent the first few hours shadowing CJ once again while he straightened up shelves, cleared aisles of clutter and dealt with customers. She enjoyed watching how he interacted with people and how easily he pulled them into conversation. Granted, that was what they were paid to do. Nancy had stressed, numerous times, the importance of prioritizing patrons. But she got the sense that, to CJ, this was more than a job. He had such a genuine love for people.

She admired that about him.

CJ laughed about something, and she refocused on him and the older gentleman he was helping. The man had a thick white beard with a center streak of black, eyes the color of coal and a large, slightly crooked nose.

"I hear you." CJ pulled a plastic-wrapped air filter from the shelf. "These gas prices have me seriously considering buying a motorcycle."

The man chuckled. "Doubt you'll find a better excuse to tell the missus."

CJ's gaze pinged to Harper's, a hint of sadness shadowing his eyes. But then his easy smile returned. "Want to ring Mr. Huxley up for me?"

"Sure."

The three of them walked to the front and CJ placed the man's item on the counter, him standing in front of the cash register while she and CJ moved behind it.

"Did you find everything okay?" Her cheeks heated at the absurdity of her question, considering she and CJ had been helping the gentleman only moments prior. "I mean, is there anything else you need?"

"Nope." He pulled a tattered wallet from his back pocket and flipped it open. "I'm right as rain and wouldn't have it any other way."

She laughed. "All right then." She rang him up, swiped his card and handed him his receipt. "Have a great day, sir."

"It already has been, little lady." He winked and, with his purchase under his arm, strolled out whistling a tune she didn't recognize.

CJ turned to her with a smile. "You're a pro." He glanced at his phone. "I've got to leave soon to meet a buddy who'll be doing some church repairs. We shouldn't be too busy. Think you can finish up shelving our returns while I'm gone?"

"Sure." Hopefully, he didn't expect her to work quickly without him there to direct her. She still wasn't all that familiar with where they kept things, especially when it came to the tools section. She didn't even know what half of them were.

Harper spent the next couple of hours walking up and down the aisles, searching the pictures displayed on various items and their specifications with what was printed on the shelf stickers. There'd been a few times when she'd finally given up and asked Ken for help, only to learn the light bulbs or extension cord or whatever she'd been searching for had been in plain view the entire time.

She sensed Ken was beginning to get frustrated, which is why she was trying so hard to lift an eighty-pound bag of cement, one of four piled along the wall, onto the rolling cart. But no amount of pushing and grunting budged the thing.

With a huff, she went, once again, in search of her irritated coworker. She found him helping a customer in plumbing. He glanced up as she approached, frowned and then refocused on the short, broad-shouldered man standing in front of him. Apparently, the guy had a clogged main drain that was causing backup in his sink and bathrooms.

Ken crossed one arm over his chest and widened his stance. "Before you do anything, make sure to shut off your water and let it all drain out overnight. Otherwise, you're going to have a mess on your hands. If your nut's corners have been rounded off, file it square, so you can grip it with a pipe wrench. You got one of those?"

The man nodded.

Ken tipped up the bill of his cap. "'Cause if not, we've got a bunch of our tools on sale for 15 percent off."

This launched a discussion on other discounts, current and upcoming, which then morphed into a conversation on rising inflation and its negative effect on farmers. She contemplated leaving to find a more productive use of her time, but she'd put away everything she could lift on her own and CJ hadn't given her any other tasks before he'd left. Instead, she occupied herself by scanning the contraptions displayed on either side of her in an attempt to remember the location for each.

She felt like she was back in anatomy class, only swapping studying bones, muscles and veins for faucet stems, cartridges and steel repair clamps.

Her hopes of gaining Ken's attention once he and the man finished talking clogs and poorly installed plumbing were dashed when he led the man to the cash register without a sideways glance her way. By the time the guy left, she felt even more like an inconvenience, thanks in part to Ken's tense expression.

"You need something?" His tone revealed his irritation.

"Yes, if you have a minute." She told him about the heavy bags she'd been unable to lift.

He released a breath and marched over to where they temporarily stored returns.

She hurried after him, confused by his sudden change in behavior. He hadn't been this prickly the day before. Had something happened? She told herself his mood wasn't about her, but he'd acted pleasant enough to the man with the plumbing issue. Then again, he'd been a customer. It made sense Ken would don a helpful persona.

He tossed the bags, one after the other, onto the rolling cart as if they were little more than overstuffed pillows.

"Thank you." She grabbed the cart's handles.

Dusting off his hands, he gave a quick nod and started to leave.

"Excuse me?"

He turned back around, eyebrow quirked.

"Can you help me place these back on the shelves, please?"

He eyed her for a moment. "This is a physical job. You sure you're up for it?"

She swallowed and, picking at her pinkie nail, dropped her gaze. Then, taking a deep breath, looked up once again only to see him pushing the cart toward the garden department.

She caught up with him at the seed display.

Ken glanced over his shoulder. "I got this. You go do whatever else you've got to do."

Had she done something to upset him? This was the last place to start creating enemies. CJ and his mom had just started warming up to her. She didn't need Ken, a man who probably carried a great deal of influence here, to start poking at recently settled emotions.

Harper spent the next hour roaming the store, straightening and doing her best to familiarize herself with all the products. But she couldn't help but feel as if she was wasting the hourly wage Nancy paid her. What if she determined Harper wasn't useful enough and cut her loose?

Then she'd find something else and remain focused on her goal. She'd risen above numerous challenges over the years. She could certainly overcome whatever present hurdles stood between her and her dreams.

CJ walked in at a quarter to three, carrying a grocery bag in one hand and a leftover container in the other. "Hey." His grin gave Harper's heart a slight lurch. "How'd things go while

I was gone? The walls still standing?" He looked about. "Ceiling didn't fall. That's a good sign."

Anxiety tempered her laugh, her interaction with Ken and the hour of inefficiency that had followed still fresh on her mind. "If that's your definition of a great workday, I'd say I rocked it."

He pulled his phone from his back pocket and glanced at his screen. "You ready to clock out for the day?"

"Okay."

As she followed him to the break room, he asked questions about her afternoon while he was away. Had she had any difficulties? Had they been busy? Did she get any time on the cash register?

Taking her time card, she shook her head. "Ken rang everybody up." Not knowing the answers to anyone's questions, she'd mainly hung back and let him tend to whoever had come in. Hopefully, she'd become more useful once her understanding of Nuts, Bolts and Boards grew. Yet she'd never gain the experience and knowledge that he, CJ and CJ's parents had. Nor would she be able to lift eighty-pound bags of cement like Ken.

His question replayed through her mind. *This is a physical job. You sure you're up for it?* A physical job where people wanted to know everything from how to regrout tile to how to build a deck, activities she hadn't a clue about.

Maybe she wasn't the best person for this position, but she was here, and she needed the paycheck. She'd do her best for as long as the Jenkinses allowed. If they ended up cutting her loose, she'd move to plan B.

More accurately, she'd create a plan to move on to.

CJ crossed to the fridge, opened it, then glanced at his to-go. "Might as well take this home with me and leave my lunch for tomorrow." He closed the door and turned to her.

"You're leaving now?" She had somehow assumed he'd work through the evening. Understanding how demanding small business ownership could be, she liked thinking that maybe he was able to catch some free time.

"Yep. I try to watch my hours."

Apparently, he'd learned how to set boundaries, something he'd struggled with in the past. They'd both grown up since their high school days.

She retrieved her purse from one of the lockers. "You free tonight?"

His eyes widened and he simply stared at her for an extended moment.

Heat rushed to her face. Did he think she was asking him on a date? She spoke quickly on an exhale. "To practice for the chain-saw carving event."

His face relaxed. "Oh. Sure." He hesitated. "You don't work at the library?"

"Not until 4:00 p.m. tomorrow. Although, I might need to bring Emaline with me." Her mom had talked about wanting to make candles to sell with her other home-crafted items at the farmers market—her way of "supplementing her sporadic employment." An endeavor that, from Harper's perspective, didn't bring in enough to justify the time and expense, not that this was any of her concern. She had enough to worry about keeping herself employed.

"Then, yeah, I can do that." He grinned. "I really appreciate the help, and you can bring your daughter, no problem. I could use a dash of cuteness in my day."

She laughed, grateful for his acceptance. "What time should I come over?" She accompanied him as he strolled down the hall and toward the front of the store. She sensed Ken watching her from where he stood near the cash register. She offered a slight smile and wave, receiving a quick nod in return.

CJ raised a hand in goodbye then opened and held the door for her. "Come on by whenever. I'll be there."

As she stepped past him, a gentle breeze carried his sage, leather and apple scent toward her, alerting her to his nearness. It reminded her of the sense of comfort, safety and acceptance she'd always felt whenever they'd been together.

Harper had missed that connection. She'd never found a replacement, and not for lack of trying. She'd dated a few people in Seattle, some healthier and more mature than others, before finally falling for Emaline's biological dad. He'd seemed so attentive, so charming, and he had been. But, unfortunately, not just to her.

She adjusted her purse strap draped over her shoulder, suddenly feeling shy and uncertain. "I need to run home and grab Emaline. Give me thirty minutes?"

A spark lit his eyes then faded behind the professional expression she'd seen him don for customers. "Sounds great."

Once in her car, she sat with both hands on the steering wheel and released a heavy breath. *Harper Moore, what are you doing?*

She could not, would not, fall for CJ again. Their lives were headed in completely different directions, and she'd already sacrificed way too much for her dream for her to abandon it now. Otherwise, all her hard work, the hours of rehearsals, bruised feet, sprained ankles and sleepless nights spent stressing over that last open slot would be wasted.

Shifting her thoughts to her daughter, she clicked on her car radio and eased onto Main Street.

She entered her house to the smell of melted wax, cinnamon, and the sound of eighties' rock. Emaline was in the baby swing, which had stopped swinging.

Harper dropped her purse on the ground and hurried across the room. "Hey, sweet girl." She unfastened her daughter's straps, picked her up and pulled her close to her chest. "How long have you been in there?"

"Are you implying I'm neglecting my granddaughter?" her mom said from the kitchen entrance.

She sounded frustrated. Had she had a bad day?

Her mom wore a red floral T-shirt and her hair pulled back with a wide cotton headband. Her eyes still carried the smudges from yesterday's mascara.

"I didn't mean to sound ungrateful." Harper did, however, worry that Emaline might be spending too much time occupying herself. But she was probably just being an overprotective, nervous mother.

Hand acting as a seat, she faced her daughter outward, back to her chest, and bounced her way into the kitchen. Blue hobnail glass jars and bags of wax lined the counter next to a stack of wicks. On the stove, her mom's metal candle pitcher centered a large steaming pot.

"You've been busy." She glanced around, craving something citrusy. Not finding anything, she pulled a box of crackers from the cupboard and poured some into a mug.

"Building up my merchandise. Folks didn't seem to like the sage much, so I decided to try foodie scents."

For her sake, Harper hoped she was right. Otherwise, her mom would soon be adding to the boxes of unsold goods clogging the garage.

She suspected there'd soon come a time when her mom would be forced to admit the obvious— Sage Creek had more crafters, and many of them quite talented, than purchasers.

That seemed to be CJ's struggle as well. Although he was incredibly talented, not everyone appreciated the time and skill that went into creating a piece of art. If his desire to make it as a carver felt anything like hers for dancing, then she could understand how important this upcoming contest must feel.

After the pain she'd cost him chasing after her dream, it felt somewhat redemptive to think she could play a part in him reaching his. That was the only reason she'd volunteered to help—not because she'd wanted to spend more time with him. She was already doing enough of that as it was. She could feel her emotional resolve to remain detached from the man who had once been her entire world weaken.

When CJ got home, he checked on his horses then jumped in the shower. He was in the middle of tidying up his house when he heard a car approach. He took his morning dishes from the coffee table to the sink, along with his plate and silverware from supper, and returned a bag of chips and half a loaf of bread to the cupboard.

Glancing at the overfilled garbage can that he should have emptied the day before, he grabbed the papers with contest information and pictures printed off the internet and hustled outside.

Harper was removing Emaline from her car seat. She wore the same formfitting jeans and V-necked T-shirt she'd worn to work, only without the vest. She'd also let her hair down, and her wavy locks, streaked with a hint of red, stirred in the breeze.

A memory resurfaced of him sifting his hands through her silky hair, releasing the soft scent of her shampoo. Back then, she'd smelled like jasmine. Now she smelled like an enticing mixture of pineapple and coconut. It reminded him of lazy summer afternoons sitting on a gently swaying porch swing, the wind stirring his mama's flowers extending from the stairs both ways for the length of the house.

He came to her side with a smile that felt much too big. "Hey. Thanks for coming."

"Of course."

"You, too, little one." He held out an index finger and wiggled it when she grabbed it. "You come to help your mama toss out impossible challenges?"

The child's face lit up.

He chuckled. "You are, huh? That's why you came?" What was it about babies that could turn a man's voice singsongy? He looked at Harper once again. "I have a feeling your little cutie will be a mite distracting."

She laughed. "I have that problem on occasion." She kissed her daughter's neck, triggering a delighted squeal. "Emaline is by far the best thing to happen to me."

She'd once said the same thing about him.

Why did his thoughts keep drifting to the past? Those days were over and, had you asked him a month ago, he would've said forgotten. Well, mostly forgotten, except for those unexpected memories that reminded him of the love they'd once shared.

Back then, he'd felt certain nothing would come between them.

"Would you like to hold her?" Harper asked.

"Huh?" He swallowed. He hadn't held a little one since Harper's babysitting days, and he'd made the baby cry.

"She won't break. Promise."

"Um…okay." He set his pages on the ground and extended his arms, hands up. Muscles tensing, he waited for her to place Emaline in the crook of his bent elbows.

"Relax and hold her to you."

He did, warmth and an odd paternal pull washing over him as he cradled her soft little body against his chest. She smelled like strawberry, milk and fresh bread.

Making a gurgling noise, she bounced, her chubby arm smacking him in the face before her fist found her mouth.

Peering down on her, he laughed. "That must taste awfully good. Think I can get a nibble?" He brought her other hand to his lips and mouthed it, eliciting a contagious giggle. "Just one more bite?" He did it again, unable to contain his grin. He glanced at Harper, his attention snagged by the intensity in her eyes.

She was looking at him with the same expression, the same focus, as she often had back when they'd been dating.

He cleared his throat, returned her daughter and picked up his papers. "So, how should we do this?" He handed her the top page—a copy of various carving challenges he'd ferreted out online.

She scanned the sheet and shrugged. "I'm guessing during the competition, the judges give you a certain amount of time to create something that fits particular themes?"

"Yep."

"How about I do something similar. Might help prepare you to think and carve in a high-pressure situation."

"Sounds effectively stressful." He chuckled and led the way to his shop. As he muscled open the wide sliding door and flicked on the light, the scent of cedar, shellac and lacquer wafted to him.

Harper came up behind him. "What's this going to be?" She stepped up to a partially finished—then abandoned—statue of an octopus.

"A mistake." He laughed and explained his intentions. "A tentacle broke off and I need to mend it."

"What about these?" She pointed to three eagles mounted on stumps.

"Need to do the detail feather work on those." He pointed out other pieces, some awaiting wax or paint, others with cracks he needed to repair. "And those little jewels growing cobwebs in that corner—" he pointed "—are bursts of inspiration I haven't finished."

"How many hours a week do you spend carving?"

He shrugged. "Depends on the week and what all I've got going on." In some ways, this space was evidence of his largely nonexistent social life. His closest friends were all married with kids, and there wasn't anyone he'd felt interested in dating.

Until now.

But that wasn't why she was here—in Sage Creek or his workshop.

Shucking the thought, he grabbed his chain saw, the partially filled gasoline can, and slipped back outside. "So, what's my first challenge?"

"Hmm…" She tapped a finger against her lips. The lips he'd kissed countless times. "I know. Ocean meets land."

"What does that mean?"

She smiled. "You tell me."

"Right." He crossed one arm over his chest, clasped his elbow in one hand and scratched his jaw with the other. "First thought is waves, maybe a dolphin with rocky cliffs behind, but I doubt that's unique enough to get much traction."

"How about we do some word associations." She sat on a thick section of trunk lying on the ground. "I'll say something, like water, then you say the next object that pops into your head, then I will, then you, and so forth."

"Okay."

"Water."

"Waves."

"Mermaid."

"Coral."

"Sunken treasure."

"Pirates."

They continued for a few minutes before she said, "What if you put a few of those together?"

He sifted through a series of ideas, some more plausible than others, but at least a handful with plenty of grabability. "I'll have to try this exercise more often."

Regardless of how he did in the contest, or if the judges even invited him to compete in the master's class, he could come up with highly original pieces to sell collectors. And one day, he *would* have collectors seeking out his stuff. Even if it took him decades to reach that level of notoriety.

Her grin lit up her face. "Yeah? You found it helpful?"

"I did. In fact, I think I know what I want to make."

"Awesome." She held out Emaline. "Can you take her for a minute?"

"Um, sure? Although, I might create better results if I kept my hands infant-free."

She rolled her eyes. "Hilarious. Just give me a second to get her set up."

He rested his chain saw against the outside of

his shed and took the baby, then waited while Harper unloaded numerous items from her vehicle, including a playpen, toys and a video camera. "Wow. You came prepared."

"Just hoping to bring her home with all of her fingers and toes intact."

"Smart."

One hand on her hip, she glanced back toward her car. "I brought my ring light. They're easier to transport than those big LEDs photographers use and usually get the job done. But with the sun being out and all, I don't think we'll need it."

He raised an eyebrow. "You one of those social media influencers or something?"

She laughed. "Hardly. I take clips of me dancing. When companies want video auditions."

He frowned at the reminder of her plans to leave Sage Creek. "I see."

He spent the next hour carving while she alternated between taking photos and video clips with her phone and entertaining her daughter. Had Harper not been there, he probably would've kept at it until dusk, but he was probably starting to bore her.

Starting? She'd probably reached that state long ago. Not to mention, it was getting near suppertime.

He set his chain saw aside and brushed dust from his hands and hair. "You hungry?"

Her eyebrows shot up and, for a moment, she seemed unsure how to respond. But then her expression relaxed into a soft smile. "I am, actually."

"How about I grill us some steaks?"

"That sounds wonderful."

And just like that, he'd extended their evening and turned it from something obviously platonic into what could easily become romantic.

If they let it. But he had no intention of doing that, and she hadn't showed anything other than a casual, friendly interest in him, if that.

In fact, Harper was probably only here out of obligation, still feeling like she had to pay him back in some way, first for him fixing her car, then for the job. And maybe, if he reminded himself of how uninterested she was, he wouldn't fall in love with her all over again. Although he was beginning to fear it was too late for that.

Chapter Eight

Harper centered herself with a deep breath. The prospect of sitting across a table from CJ spiked her pulse. She couldn't think of anything more romantic than sharing a meal with the man she'd once loved so deeply, except perhaps to be sharing one that he himself had cooked. Had he always been this thoughtful?

Holding Emaline, he glanced over his shoulder at her playpen. "Need me to help you with anything?"

The fact that he didn't immediately try to return her daughter, and the way his eyes softened whenever he glanced down at her, made Harper think perhaps he felt reluctant to do so.

"I've got it." Gathering her daughter's blanket, diaper bag and toys would give her time to manage her emotions.

What had she just agreed to? Accepting his

dinner invite might not have been such a horrible idea, if her insides didn't practically melt to mush whenever he turned his green eyes her way. Or, if she wasn't growing increasingly attached to him, her internal reactions creeping toward pre-breakup intensity. Or, if seeing him holding his chain saw, his thick brows pinched in concentration, his biceps flexing, hadn't almost made her regret walking away five years ago.

Almost. She'd made the right decision, for them both. Regardless of how things had turned out for her—temporarily—she'd been able to tour with a professional dance company. And in her absence, CJ had birthed a dream. She could tell by watching him that carving made him feel alive in much the same way dance did her. Had she stayed, his constant focus on her could've kept him from discovering his passion for carving.

And now? They both kept moving—him toward becoming a successful artist and her toward returning to the stage. Saying goodbye, again, would hurt. But they'd healed before and would do so again.

With a sigh, she placed a handful of Emaline's sensory toys back into her diaper bag alongside her folded Noah's ark blanket, draped the strap over her shoulder and climbed CJ's steps. He'd left the front door open and his deep voice drifting through the screen caused her heart to stutter.

He was singing! Stepping inside, she paused to make out the song, then suppressed a giggle.

Harper smiled and leaned a shoulder against the door frame separating the living room from the kitchen. "That's a lullaby I've not heard before. What's it called?"

A hint of pink settled into his face. "It's *The Green Berets* movie theme song."

She quirked an eyebrow at him. "Quite soothing and whimsical, I'm sure."

He laughed. "She looked like she was about to fuss, and those were the only lyrics I could think of."

"*About* to fuss, huh? Must have been terrifying." How easily she was falling back into their old teasing banter. Was that a sign of friendship or further indication that her heart was inching in a forbidden direction?

He gave a one-shoulder shrug and turned toward his cupboards, her daughter looking quite content tucked between his chest and arm.

Either Harper had hurt him or he, too, had sensed their precarious footing—an indication that he'd closed his heart to her as firmly as she was trying to close hers to him.

She came up beside him and placed a hand on his shoulder, a surge of warmth shooting through her upon contact. "I was just teasing. Would you like me to take her?"

He glanced at Emaline with a look of wonder in his eyes. "I don't mind."

Maybe she was reading too much into this, but she sensed he wanted to say no. Funny, he'd always been great with kids—the way he used to get the children she babysat laughing! But she never remembered him looking at them with the almost paternal fondness with which she'd caught him gazing at Emaline.

Thinking this way would only make it harder when it came time for her to leave.

Gently bouncing the little one, cradled one-handedly against his opposite shoulder, he moved to the fridge, opened it and stared inside for a moment. "Although... I probably shouldn't get raw meat juice on her." He rotated to reveal his adorable easy grin, made all the more charming by the disarming display of both strength and tenderness.

Unable to contain the smile that seemed to erupt from somewhere deep in her soul, Harper extended her arms. "Come here, sweet pea." She kissed her temple, then her nose and, after swaying with her for a few moments, retrieved her blanket from her diaper bag.

Midway through spreading it across the floor, she glanced back at the archway leading to the tidy but not babyproof living room, thankful Emaline hadn't yet learned to crawl. But she wouldn't remain occupied on her back long.

"Excuse me for a sec." She darted back outside and returned with her daughter's stroller, placed a few animal-shaped teething rings on the tray and clipped the activity toy to the raised handle. Emaline loved batting at the hanging rattle.

CJ watched with an amused glint in his eye as she fastened Emaline in. "Transportable confinement. Smart."

"She actually loves this thing, probably because it lets her see what's going on."

"And allows you a quick getaway, should I botch the meal?"

Although she knew he spoke in jest, his words felt a bit too apropos. Only, not because of any outcome in relation to the steaks, but rather the inner resolve his grilling, and this evening in general, threatened to weaken.

Covering her vulnerability with a laugh that came out too high-pitched, Harper lifted her chin and strode to his cupboards. "Want me to make a side?"

"You can try. But I must warn you, I don't have much. I'd say I need to hit the grocery, which technically would be accurate. The truth of the matter is, I tend to survive on frozen meals and snack items." He pulled out a package of meat wrapped in butcher paper, unwrapped it and placed it on a flat baking sheet.

"Typical bachelor." She rolled her eyes with feigned annoyance. "Yet you have steak."

"Always." He chuckled. "Well, almost. Buy half a cow from a rancher buddy every now and again. Best beef I've tasted."

"I'm in for a treat then." She grabbed a can of mushrooms and a couple packages of Top Ramen from his cupboards then moved to the fridge, which was heavy on condiments and light on most everything else. Harper picked up a rather large bunch of kale and turned to him, amused. "Why do I feel like there's a story behind this?"

He laughed. "An older lady brought that into the store as a way to thank us for repairing a few of her windows."

"For free?" She carried the vegetable to his sink.

CJ gave a slight shrug and set a handful of spices, some brown sugar and vinegar on the counter. "Her husband was one of our most loyal—and friendly—customers. I remember him coming in as far back as my kindergarten year, and always with a sucker or piece of gum for me. On Christmas, he and his wife always brought us a pie of some sort, and often a small gift for me. A few years ago, he suddenly stopped coming in. After a while, my folks got worried, so went out to his place."

"Do you have a cutting board I can use?"

He nodded, rummaged through a bottom shelf near his knee and handed one over, made, not surprisingly, from two shades of wood, along with a chef's knife.

"Thanks." She started slicing the stems from the kale. "Regarding the couple—how'd your parents know where they lived?"

"Phone book, an old delivery invoice? Asking around?"

"Right. Sometimes I forget how close-knit this town is."

"One of the things I love about it."

He covered the steaks with the spice-brown-sugar mixture he'd stirred together with a dash of vinegar and oil.

"You made your own marinade?" she asked. "I'm impressed."

"Stole the recipe from my dad. Anyway, back to your question, my parents arrived at that couple's place to find the lawn overgrown, the house dark, and Mrs. Shaw was just sort of... I don't remember how my parents described it, but their basic interpretation was that she'd given up."

"Did they have kids?"

He shook his head. "That was probably why Mr. Shaw took such interest in me."

"Poor thing. She must have felt so alone."

"And hopeless. Least, that was my mom's fear. So, she convinced my dad to convince her that her husband had purchased lifetime handyman service. The way they figured it, this wasn't dishonest, because he'd spent enough of his hard-earned dollars at Nuts, Bolts and Boards to qualify him for such a thing, had it existed. Plus, it just seemed the right thing to do."

Harper had heard him and his parents use that phrase countless times back when they'd been dating. While she'd always admired their sense of town member loyalty, she could now see this was obviously a core family trait, perhaps one passed down for generations.

What moral characteristics was she actively instilling in Emaline?

Maybe her need for church extended beyond making good on her promise to God.

"I better go fire up the grill." CJ moved to the sink to wash his hands. "Probably should've done that first thing."

While he dashed out through the kitchen door she assumed led to his back porch or yard, she chopped the kale, turned it, then began chopping again. He returned, a hint of charcoal merging with his familiar sage, apple and leather scent.

He came up behind her, his breath warm on the back of her neck. "Need any help?"

"No." Did her strong, rapid response disclose her nervousness? She took in a deep breath and released it slowly. "But thank you."

Behind them, Emaline cooed and babbled.

He chuckled and turned around. "Well, then, if you don't need me, how about I spend some time with this little nugget?" He pivoted a chair to face her, sat and pulled her stroller closer. "What do you think, princess? Does that sound okay to you?"

She was touched by the slight lilt in his voice whenever he addressed Emaline. "You can pick her up, if you want."

"Did you hear that?" He leaned forward to unbuckle her safety straps. "I'm about to break you free." He extended the last word in a whimsical tone. Settling her onto his lap, back resting against his chest, he glanced up. "You don't happen to have any of those thick books made from cloth or cardboard, do you?"

She paused midsauté to look at him. "You want to read to her?"

"Is that okay?"

"Of course. I'm just surprised."

"A couple years ago, I visited one of my cousins and her family up in Woodinville, Washington. She and her husband hadn't lived there long and hadn't found a sitter they felt comfortable with."

"I can relate to that!" She laughed. "Let me guess, you quickly found yourself filling that role."

"I did. A bunch of their friends were going out to celebrate one of their birthdays. My cousin had originally declined, but then the kids all crashed while watching television."

"After you wore them out all day?"

He smiled. "Maybe. And myself, which is why it made sense to us all for them to slip out for a bit. For the first hour or so, everything was fine. I didn't hear a peep out of them. But then their toddler had a nightmare and started hollering loud enough to wake the neighbors—and the baby."

She covered a giggle with her hand. "Oh, no."

"Oh, yes. And it gets worse. I hurried to comfort the two-year-old, but that only made him cry harder, demanding his mom. By this point, their youngest was wailing and the oldest—she was six—was asking me over and over where her parents were. So, here I am, holding a screaming infant, trying to comfort a toddler who was looking at me like I was the monster from his dreams, hoping their daughter, who had started to whimper, didn't lose it as well."

"Did you call the parents?"

"I tried, but their phones—both of them—kept ringing until they went to voice mail. I learned later, with a football game playing, people talking and laughing, their surroundings were pretty noisy."

"What'd you do?"

"At first, I just stood there, phone in one hand, screeching infant held in the other. But then I saw a pile of books on the floor in the living room. So, I walked over, sat on the ground, grabbed one and started to read."

"And they listened?"

"Not at first. Pretty sure they couldn't hear me above all their carrying on. They were near burst-your-eardrums loud."

"I can imagine!"

"Eventually, they grew curious, or maybe their voices grew tired, I don't know. The two older ones started inching toward me, the sister first. Pretty soon, she was close enough to rub the back of her littlest brother's head. 'He likes this one,' she said, picking up a thick, cardboard-type book with colorful animals on the cover."

"That's so precious."

"This gave the toddler the courage to nestle in. By the time my cousin and her husband arrived home an hour and a half later, they were all back asleep—on me, because I was *not* moving!"

She laughed. "I imagine not." She turned the temperature on the stove burner down and faced him with a fist on her hip in mock irritation. "In regard to your question, are you worried Emaline's about to start bawling?"

"No, not at all." He spoke quickly, adorable when concerned. "I just figured—"

"I'm just teasing." She crossed the room to the diaper bag and located one cloth book and another made from plastic for the bath and brought them both to CJ. "She especially loves it when I make the animal sounds."

He blushed, his gaze dropping first to the cover then to Emaline. Clearing his throat, he straightened. "Uh, okay."

Harper watched him for a moment longer as his almost shy demeanor turned more animated with each new page. Chest warm, she returned to her stir-fry to add pepper. "The library has children's story and craft time on Tuesdays and Thursdays. I look forward to the day when I can take Emaline to those types of things."

She'd love for her daughter to have a kind, strong yet tender father figure like CJ in her life one day, as well. Too bad he'd always remain so tied to Sage Creek, and that she couldn't do what she loved most, should she stay.

CJ poked his head through the back door, the aroma of apple, garlic and mesquite wafting over him and causing his stomach to rumble. "Want to eat out here on the deck? It's shaded, and there's a nice breeze blowing, so it's not suffocatingly hot." Not to mention, mail, rough sketches, a chunk of wood and various hand-carving tools cluttered his kitchen table.

From the stove, Harper glanced over her shoulder. First at him and then at Emaline, who babbled in her stroller, then back to him. "That sounds lovely." She opened a couple cupboards in front of her. "Do you have a serving dish?"

"How about we dish ourselves up in here." He closed the air vents and lid to his grill and stepped inside.

"Efficient." She smiled and scooped a spoonful of ramen stir-fry onto two plates.

"I'll take those so you can grab little miss."

"Thanks." She handed over the dishes then followed him out, pushing Emaline's stroller, which she rolled to the wooden picnic table. "This was one of the best investments I've made as a mom. Stroller, car seat, grocery cart when needed." She motioned to the basket underneath Emaline's seat. "And a portable high chair."

"Brilliant." Steaming steaks distributed, he darted back inside to make a pitcher of lemonade from a powder mix, then returned with it and two glasses. "Hope you're not craving sweet tea."

She sat kitty-corner to her daughter. "Nope. I'm just happy for the food." She laughed.

Her response concerned him. "This probably isn't any of my business, but are you doing all right?"

"I'm not starving or anything, although I am learning to stretch my buck, as they say." She explained an upcoming change in her living arrangement with her parents. "I found a website where you can type in a list of whatever you have on hand, and they'll pull up a series of recipes." She handed Emaline a glittery pink sippy cup.

He swallowed a mouthful of surprisingly good noodles. "Is that how you came up with the idea for this?" He pointed at the stir-fry. "Because it's amazing."

"Really?"

About to take a drink, he nodded. "Might need to send me a link." Although what he'd love even more would be for her to come over again so they could cook—and eat—together. He knew his thoughts, and his heart, were treading on shaky turf, but he wasn't sure he cared.

"You do know you actually need some groceries to work with, right? Besides ketchup packets, I mean."

"Ouch." He placed a fist to his chest in mock offense. "You wound me."

"Oh, I'm sure." She plopped a slice of steak into her mouth, closed her eyes and gave a soft moan. "This is seriously amazing."

"Got more in my freezer just waiting to get fired up. Come over anytime."

Her eyes widened slightly, as if she'd read the deeper invitation beneath his casual words. But then she pulled a small jar filled with something orange from her diaper bag and shifted toward her daughter. "I almost feel mean feeding you mushy squash now." She turned to CJ. "Except that she loves it—along with pureed peas, turkey and carrots."

"Delicious, I'm sure." Memories swept over him as he watched her interact with her daughter. "Do you remember the day you were babysitting for the Morenos and you thought someone had snuck into their basement?"

She giggled. "And how you turned all knight-in-shining-armor, creeping down the stairs wielding a frying pan? I do."

"I admit, I may have overreacted a bit."

"You think?" Amusement danced in her eyes. "Either that or you'd watched too many slapstick cartoons."

"But I also seem to remember someone telling the kids y'all were playing hide-and-seek so that you could convince them to cram into the cupboards above the washing machine and dryer."

"Hey, now. I was just trying to keep them safe."

"From a stray cat." Their shared laughter reminded him of all the times they'd connected over humor. Harper could be serious and determined, especially when pursuing a goal. But she could be loads of fun as well. The type of person able to brighten even the most frustrating or discouraging days.

He'd missed this. Missed her.

CJ hated thinking that she was having a difficult time financially and hoped working at the hardware store helped. But a little struggle wasn't all bad, if it kept her from saving up whatever she needed to return to Seattle.

If it kept her here, in Sage Creek, with him.

The longer she stayed, the more time he had to win her heart—for good.

Chapter Nine

The next day, with extra time before she needed to leave for the library, Harper sat at the kitchen table with her laptop open before her. The whiff of hazelnut rising from her heavily doctored coffee merged with the lingering aroma of barbecued chicken and melted Swiss from lunch. She smiled at her mom's off-key voice as she rocked and sang to Emaline in the living room.

Moving back home, and all that had precipitated it, had cut deeply, and living under her mom's roof once again certainly wasn't easy. But it did come with priceless benefits, like the fact that her daughter was getting so much time with her grandmother.

If only Sage Creek had more of a dance community, then maybe Harper could stay. But she couldn't let go of her dream.

What if she found a choreographer's job in Houston? Then she could see CJ on the weekends.

She frowned. Obviously, she was falling for the man; the one thing she'd determined *not* to do. Their lives were heading in completely different directions.

Right?

Could he, would he, follow her, whether to Seattle, Houston or whatever city offered her the career she'd spent her life working toward?

Highly unlikely. He may have found his passion, but he remained precisely where she'd left him—tied to this place and his parents' store.

Was that the root of her frustration? The reason she'd not been able to commit to him, to promise the rest of her life to him, years ago? Because she'd known, if it came down to it, he'd choose his parents' business over her. Just as her dad had chosen his job and, ultimately, whatever had appealed to him most in the moment, over her mom—only to leave her scrambling to make ends meet, raising her daughter alone, with a half-earned college degree?

With a huff, Harper refocused on her internet job search. Forty-five minutes later, she'd sent her résumé and some video clips to five companies. Later, she'd need to record some new videos for her Instagram account. Although a lot of places still conducted live auditions, they often spent time checking out applicants online. Social media was quickly becoming a vital dance portfolio.

She eyed the clock and stood with a moan. "Apparently, time flies when you're trying to plan your life."

Her mom glanced around Emaline, who stood, bouncing in her lap. "You heading to work?"

She nodded, grabbed her sacked dinner from the fridge and, entering the living room, her purse and water bottle from the coffee table. "Thank you for watching Miss Princess for me. Again." She ran a hand over her daughter's silky-fine hair and kissed her cheek.

"You know I love it."

"I do, and I'm really grateful for all of your help." Lack of dependable and affordable child-care had been her biggest challenge in Seattle. Next time she signed with a dance company, in any capacity, she'd make sure they paid enough for her and Emaline to live on. Maybe even spring for a movie or lunch out occasionally.

Until then, she'd juggle her job schedules and save every possible penny.

Harper arrived at the library to find each parking space in front and in the small lot behind full. Inside, children of varied ages darted about while moms, some dressed in exercise pants, others in trendy outfits, chatted with one another. One woman wearing a purple T-shirt and jeans, her frizzy red hair barely contained in a messy bun, scampered after a toddler pulling books from the shelves.

At the checkout desk, Harper paused and made eye contact with Ruby. "I take it Dynamo the Dragon was a hit?" That character, and the books and now cartoons from which he'd come, had become quite popular, which was why their boss had planned today's event—a craft, dress up, sing songs deal—themed after the program.

"If by hit, you mean crazy and chaotic, then yes." Ruby laughed. "But don't worry, the rest of the night should be pretty quiet. Saltwater Taffy is playing at the lake."

Harper groaned. "Live music, and we're stuck here?"

"You could've requested tonight off."

Except that she really needed the money. "I doubt Elise would've given it to me."

"Considering she's not here and we are, you're probably right."

Harper laughed. "Any other fun social stuff coming up I should know about?" She spent way too many of her off hours at home. Except for the times she'd gone to CJ's—something she could easily get used to. She smiled as an image of him singing *The Green Berets* song to Emaline came to mind. Then she reminded herself of their ultimate trajectories—him here, her not.

"Check the community board." Ruby crumpled a sticky note and tossed it into the nearby wastebasket. "People are always pinning stuff up. Spaghetti feeds. Charity functions. Lost pets. Horses for sale…"

"Well, now, that sounds useful. For that stable sitting empty in my mother's massive backyard."

"Pretty sure CJ would take you riding, if you asked." Ruby wiggled her brows.

"Stop." She turned and marched toward the employee break room before her coworker could see the heat flooding her face.

Although, the idea was appealing. Too appealing for her, or her goal's, good.

With a sigh, she set her dinner in the fridge and walked out, pausing to scan the corkboard she'd walked by dozens of times. She'd never paid much attention to the numerous flyers, posters and note cards attached to it. Most of what she read didn't interest her. She didn't need a Realtor or lawyer, and couldn't afford a housekeeper or a babysitter for that matter. Nor did she have a place to board a broodmare.

Harper started to leave when a burst of color caught her eye. Refocusing on the glossy pages in front of her, she read the bold letters printed in blue, red, yellow and orange. Little Tykes, a place she'd always wanted to check out but had never had the funds to visit, was offering a two-for-one special. While that would certainly stretch her finances, it seemed too good a deal to pass up. And if the claims made by the ad were true, the activities would help stimulate Emaline's brain development.

Regardless of what those classes entailed, they would give her something to do other than binge-watch rom-coms.

Maybe she'd even find an in with the local moms, a group that seemed so connected with one another but not exactly open to her. Probably, in part, because of her over-the-top bragging when she'd received admittance into one of the most prestigious dance universities in Seattle. But that had been over five years ago. She'd grown a lot since then.

Humility had a way of maturing a person.

Maybe the Little Tykes deal would provide her an opportunity to demonstrate how much she'd changed. The next class was tomorrow morning. She checked her phone calendar, equally relieved and nervous to discover she was off. Considering Trisha was practically her only friend, unless one counted those in her former dance community with whom she shared social media "likes," she absolutely needed to go. But she wasn't looking forward to encountering any of the ladies who seemed to exchange raised-eyebrow whispers whenever she came around.

Regardless, Harper had never allowed the

"keepers of the cliques" to intimidate her in high school, nor did she intend to start doing so now.

She took a picture of the advertisement and traipsed back up front, feeling considerably cheered to tackle the ever-full return carts.

"What's got you all smiley today?"

She turned to find Lucy, someone of whom she'd grown quite fond, standing before her, wearing a blue-and-white-striped cotton dress and large sunshine earrings.

Harper smiled. "Hello, ma'am."

"How's your sweet baby? Growing like a weed, I imagine?"

"About."

"Figured she's due for another one of these." She pulled out a knit beanie that looked like a ladybug with two twisted strings poking up from the top. "And these." She handed over a matching bib and booties.

"They're adorable!" And must have taken her hours. "You didn't have to do this."

"Fiddling with yarn soothes me." She winked. "And making stuff for your little one reminds me to return my horrifically overdue books. If I'm not careful, Elise will soon confiscate my card." She nodded a greeting to a short plump woman who walked past carrying a squirming, grunting toddler who clearly wanted down. Probably to join that other little guy tossing books from the shelves and onto the floor. "Speaking of reading material, do you happen to have any more copies of this book club's selection?"

"Not sure, but I can find out." She walked Lucy to the desk and repeated her question to Ruby.

When the two women launched into a conversation about the most swoonworthy heroes in print, Harper politely excused herself to tackle the filled return carts. Meandering toward the arts and recreation section, she tried to focus on the Dewey decimal system, but her thoughts kept drifting to CJ. The boyish glint in his eyes when she'd tried to pull out his creative side, followed by his intense, single-focused gaze as he'd sized up his chunk of wood, chain saw in hand.

He stood a chance at winning the carving contest. She'd love to be there when he did, and to see the look on his face when they called his name. Maybe it was because she'd helped him prepare for the competition, but she felt invested in his success.

In him.

Because she cared for him—as a friend, and nothing more.

As she slipped a how-to on abstract painting onto the shelf, another title caught her eye. Spoon carving. Interesting. Probably not something CJ would find fascinating, but he might the one next to it with patterns from the top carvers world-wide. She snapped a picture of the cover and sent it to him via text. Then waited, checking her phone obsessively for his reply.

When a customer ambled down the aisle, Harper straightened, smiled and returned to the duties her boss was paying her for. If she lingered much longer, she'd appear derelict, and she could *not* afford to get fired.

Her notifications pinged when she reached the biographies. In her hurry to respond, she nearly dropped her phone.

What in the world was wrong with her? She was acting like she'd never texted a man—who happened to be her boss, a fact she'd do well to remember—before.

With a deep breath to slow her spiked pulse, she read his text. That looks great. Check it out for me?

An image of her stopping by his place, book in hand, flashed through her mind. Frowning, she once again chastised herself for her almost comical reaction. She and CJ were friends, nothing more.

Then why had her pulse spiked at the thought of standing on his stoop, close enough to see the gray specks in his green eyes?

The next morning, having arrived at Little Tykes intentionally early, she spent nearly ten minutes driving up and down the street, debating whether she wanted to be one of the first to enter the building or to stroll in fashionably late. Unfortunately, every time she looped back around, some of her courage seeped out.

So much for leading with confidence. Seemed she'd decreased in that department since her awkward teenage years. Then again, back then, she'd felt judged because of her mom, not for what she'd feared people might be saying about her personally.

With a deep breath, Harper repeated a statement that had helped her show up to dance rehearsal, knowing she'd have to interact with her baby-denying ex. *I can do hard things.*

She parked, cut the engine and glanced at her reflection in the rearview mirror, then at her daughter, who was blowing raspberries around her fist shoved into her mouth. "Guess it's time I quit wasting gas, put on a winning smile and march in that place like the adult I am."

Grabbing the diaper bag that doubled as a purse, she stepped out and to the rear passenger's-side door. "Girl, your hair, all half an inch of it, is on point." She tapped her daughter's nose and unhooked her carrier.

Walking toward Little Tykes's single-door entrance, she made a visual sweep of the lot, trying to ignore how sharply her dilapidated vehicle stood out among its newer neighbors. She'd hoped, these classes being discounted and all, that she'd encounter a different demographic than the more affluent women who typically took their children to these types of things.

Clearly, she'd been wrong. But this was good. She'd been wanting to find a way to break into Sage Creek's mommy circle. Hopefully, this class would provide the opportunity.

With a deep breath, she burst inside with the same feigned confidence that had propelled her onto countless dance stages. A bell above her chimed, and numerous heads turned her direction, most expressions ranging from friendly to surprised. A tall brunette with mousy, shoulder-length hair parted down the middle regarded her with a scowl.

Only one out of ten openly hostile. Harper could handle that.

She made eye contact with the owner, Julia Nieves, who came into the library looking for picture books on occasion. "Sorry I'm late."

Sleek, blond hair tapered around her face, the green-eyed woman flicked a hand with a wide smile. "You're right on time." Fingertips pressed together at her waist, she addressed them all. "Welcome to Little Tykes, everyone. How many of you are first-time moms?"

A few of them, Harper included, raised their hands.

"Congrats and welcome to the beautiful world

of motherhood. How many of you are taking a Mommy-Baby Little Tykes class for the first time?"

More raised hands.

"I'm grateful to have the opportunity to introduce you to our rich, memorable, multisensory experience scientifically proven to enhance brain development." She explained how, interspersed with icebreaker questions, then directed everyone to form a circle on the polka-dotted carpet.

Harper quickly sat, her back to the long window, before her friendless status in a room full of besties became awkward. The others soon joined her on either side, legs crisscrossed, their babies in their laps.

"We'll start with some tactile tempo fun." Dressed in a jungle-print T-shirt that fit with the bright walls, Julia glided to a console on a raised shelf and upped the volume of the song playing in the background. "Grab hold of your baby's ankles and raise and lower their legs to the beat." She sashayed from person to person, arms extended and fluid, matching the lyrics about a roly-poly, rickety-pickety, silly-willy, squiggly-wiggly squirrel.

The wall to her right was painted orange with large black musical notes with smiling faces. Adjacent to that, someone had painted a mural of rolling hills, a blue sky and thick yellow beams radiating from a half-circle sun. Across from the mural, someone had painted a city made from purple, red, green and coral rectangles topped with contrasting triangles. A mess of mats, cylinder or wedged, filled the far back corner, behind which peeked a plastic wading pool filled with balls of various colors.

After they'd engaged their infants' arms and torsos in time to the music, Julia motioned for them all to stand. "Now turn your kiddo so that they face out, their back to your chest." She glanced around. "That's right. Use one hand as their seat, and with the other, hug them nice and tight around their chest. Then gently bounce as you walk about the room."

Lily, a woman who'd graduated a year after Harper, took a few lunges. "If I go deep like this, does it count as cardio training for the day?"

Her friend, a short woman with the top half of her black hair pulled back in a knot, laughed. "Girl, if you're looking to raise your heart rate, you can borrow my kindergartner anytime. I get enough steps chasing after him to last me through middle age."

"No joke." Lily huffed. "With all the running around I do, upstairs and downstairs, and everywhere in between, you'd think I'd have lost my gut by now."

Harper eyed her, noting the woman's beautiful, wavy hair, vibrant skin and infectious smile. "You look great."

Lily halted midbounce, as if momentarily caught off guard by the compliment. Then, a look of kindness filled her expression. "Thank you. That encouraged me." She angled her head. "I'd say the same about you. No one could tell that you'd ever had a watermelon-sized critter stretching your stomach."

"Right?" Her friend regarded Harper with raised eyebrows. "You a runner?"

Harper shook her head. "But I do dance, although not as much as I used to." Nor as much as she should or wanted.

She needed to stay fit in case the companies with the choreographer jobs asked for live auditions. She'd also find it easier to gain dancers' respect, and therefore cooperation, if she was able to perform the moves she prescribed.

Mauve, a former classmate who'd been silently brooding since she'd walked in, shot Harper a pointed look. "Seems you didn't turn out to be the successful ballerina you thought."

Harper fought to keep her gaze level. "I was actually into hip-hop. But yes, my plans did change. Temporarily." She could only imagine the stories about her circulating Sage Creek.

Let them talk. She'd be gone, steadily progressing toward her dream, soon enough. While

Mauve and other gossips spent the rest of their lives gabbing about how others lived theirs, Harper intended to end her days with something worth talking about.

Lily gave a slight cough and switched hands beneath her son. "My sister—she lives in Corpus Christi—she goes to one of those barre fitness classes."

Creative exercise experiences seemed to be growing in popularity. A momentary fad or ongoing trend? What did it take to run one of those establishments, anyway? Maybe, once she started her choreographer job, assuming it actually came through, Harper could work part-time at one of those fitness facilities, to gain some experience. While still devoting sufficient time with Emaline, of course.

Laughter drew her attention to three moms gathered to her left. A sense of longing welled within her as she watched the ladies interact with one another's babies. Those were the types of friends she needed. She needed to make sure to find such a community when she moved, even if it meant taking expensive mommy-baby classes.

"What's that?" Her friend bounced alongside her.

Everyone followed Lily's gaze to Harper.

She raised her chin a notch, no longer feeling like the outcast trying to muscle her way in. "It's a type of workout that combines ballet, Pilates, stretching and breathing."

Lily nodded. "My sister's super toned. Has long, lean legs and an amazing posture. After three kids."

"You know what I'd love to do?" asked a lady who'd been quiet up until then. "I'd like to try one of those ribbon classes—I think that's what they're called. Where people loop themselves around those massively long strips of fabric hanging from the ceiling."

Harper followed her gaze to the thick, exposed wooden beams above her. She loved old buildings like this one. "I did some aerial acrobatics in college."

Lily's son became fussy, so she kissed the fat folds in his neck until he began to giggle. "Was it fun?"

"It was. A great stress reliever, too." She'd chosen her first class as one of her electives then continued during open gym times for her remaining years.

Lily sighed. "Too bad we don't have anything like that here."

Harper's cell rang. Repositioning Emaline to free a hand, she pulled her phone from her back pocket and glanced at the screen.

Her breath caught and she glanced up. "Excuse me." She backed away from the group and answered. "Hey."

"Hey." His tentative tone intrigued her. "You at the library?"

"Actually, I have the day off." She told him where she was.

"That's right." He paused. "Listen, I know this is last minute, and not exactly the most exciting way to spend a Saturday night…"

Clearly, he didn't know how she spent most of her off hours. Anything he suggested would be more entertaining than ending her evening with rom-coms and a giant bowl of chocolate-mint ice cream.

The music changed to a quick-tempo song about a mother duck leading her brood over rolling hills and a stream.

She leaned a shoulder against the beam between two long windows. "What's up?"

"My parents bought tickets for the Cattle Baron's Ball."

"A fundraiser for cancer research, right?"

"Yeah. They planned on going, but then my mom got sick and my dad… He's just not the social type. Doesn't like to attend these deals alone."

"Can't say I blame him."

"Me, either. Which is sort of why I'm calling. They asked me to go, but I'd rather not show up solo…"

Her pulse spiked. Was he asking her out? "Okay?"

"Any chance you're free and up for some prime rib, live music and helping me not appear socially awkward?"

She forced a nervous laugh. "Um, as to that last part..." Hopefully her teasing tone masked her sudden breathlessness. "I'm not sure that's possible."

He went silent. Had he taken her banter as a brush-off? "What time is the event?"

"Refreshments, meet and greet starts at six thirty."

"Will I need boots and a hat?" She didn't have anything even remotely cowgirl. Thankfully, Trisha did and would be more than happy to lend a few pieces out. Unfortunately, she'd probably also bombard Harper with a plethora of questions all centered around one—were she and CJ getting back together?

Harper was beginning to wonder the same thing and wasn't sure how she felt about that.

"Does that mean you'll go?" CJ sounded pleasantly surprised, with an almost giddy undercurrent.

Harper inhaled and exhaled slowly so as not to match his tone. This wasn't a date, after all. "I'll need to make sure my mom can watch Emaline, but sure. I don't have anything better to do."

"Okay." Had her response deflated him, or was she simply detecting a relaxed, post-anxiety state?

Regardless, she would not allow this function to become more than it was—one friend supporting the other.

Both of whom once loved one another.

Why did she feel like she was tiptoeing toward the proverbial point of no return—at least, if she wanted to leave Sage Creek with her heart intact?

Chapter Ten

Not wanting to appear overly eager, CJ pulled into Harper's driveway at a quarter after six, dressed in dark jeans, a checked button-down shirt and a black vest. He'd even dusted and polished his boots, not that anyone would pay much attention to his feet.

They would be spending their night in a barn, after all. A mite fancied up, but an old farm building just the same.

Who was he kidding? Tonight was a big deal and potentially the most romantic time he'd spend with Harper since high school prom.

He feared he was falling for her all over again.

In high school, he'd loved her for her looks, determination, her wit and the fun they'd had together.

Now watching her with her daughter hit him in a deeper place.

The place where his longing for a family of his own resided.

Her front door opened. Harper emerged wearing a jean skirt that hugged her curves and hit midknee, a white cowgirl hat and a pink blouse that highlighted the beginning of a tan.

Her beauty stalled his thoughts.

But then manners shot him from his truck. He met her on the sidewalk.

Did she think he'd been sitting out here, waiting on her? He'd seen some of his more immature high school buddies acting that way, laying on their horns to "fetch" their girls. That had never been his way, not even when doing so seemed cool.

He beat her to her door and opened it for her. "You look beautiful."

With a slight blush, she fingered the pendant resting in the dimple between her collarbones. "Thanks."

She slid past him and into the seat, a faint pineapple-coconut scent floating on the air.

Clearing his throat to jolt some common sense into his muddled brain, he rounded his truck and eased in behind the wheel. He'd left the engine running, and a country music song about a lost love poured from the speakers.

He clicked it off and backed out into the road. "You been to an event at Angus Village before?"

Originally a ranch, the family had turned most of their property into a bookable venue generations ago. As the only place he knew of, apart from churches, folks could rent for parties and whatnot, it'd become a popular location for charity events, weddings and other celebrations.

She nodded. "For Haven's thirteenth birthday party." They'd both gone to school with her.

"I remember that. Wasn't that when you were dating Paul?"

"Don't remind me. I have no idea what I saw in him."

"I heard your next boyfriend was quite a step up."

She blinked as if his comment unnerved her, and he wished he could take it back.

But then she laughed. "He wasn't terrible."

He didn't know how to read her statement or whether to continue their banter or switch directions. Seemed wise to lean toward caution and not do or say anything that might make the rest of their evening painfully awkward.

And hope there'd come a day when they could speak about their emotions, past and present, more freely.

Did she even have feelings to discuss, or was she simply treating him like a friend?

What then? Could he handle being her "buddy"? Spending time with her, at this event, at work, at church—wherever they interacted now that they weren't actively avoiding one another—as little more than a pleasant companion?

Suppressing a sigh, he drove out of town and onto the two-lane highway dissecting fields and pastures.

Harper pulled a pack of gum from her purse and offered him some.

He declined.

She shrugged and popped a piece into her mouth. "I was talking to my mom about your chain-saw contest. She was impressed."

"Yeah?"

She nodded. "She even suggested we go watch. Make a girls' weekend out of it."

"Really? That's awesome."

That had to mean a lot to Harper. Back when they'd been dating, she'd cried on his shoulder numerous times about how her mom didn't seem to like her. Mrs. Moore hadn't been a terrible mom, just not always that engaged.

"Only problem, I have to work." Her tone carried a note of disappointment.

He could understand why. This might've been the first time her mother had suggested she and her daughter spend such quality time together.

Drumming his fingers on the steering wheel, he mentally reviewed the schedule. "Bet my folks could make do without you."

"You sure? On this short of notice."

"Next weekend's Principal Nguyen's retirement party."

"Meaning?"

"S'pect that'll keep most people occupied."

"You're probably right. He's a great man. Worth celebrating."

He nodded. "I'll talk with my parents."

She smiled. "Thanks."

The possibility of her coming to his event triggered a sense of giddy anticipation and anxiety.

CJ thought back to when they were teens and all the times he'd scanned the bleachers, mid football game, to catch sight of her. Each time, he'd found her standing, eyes locked on him, waving with both arms raised.

She'd never missed a game.

But back then, he'd also rarely fumbled. By the time they'd started dating, he'd felt confident in his ability to impress her on the field.

He'd felt equally sure of their relationship. He'd trusted in their love so fully, he'd never considered she might leave.

Now?

Now he realized if he wanted to reestablish what they'd once shared, he'd have to work for it. Knowing she could bail at any time.

Could this time be different? Could he somehow figure out how to hold on to her for good?

Did the fact that he was even asking himself these questions make him foolish?

Nearing the location for the ball, he followed a line of cars onto a winding gravel road lined with blooming myrtle trees growing in a long stretch of wildflowers. Beyond, fields of tall, waving grass grew in each direction.

This soon gave way to a vehicle-covered field on the right, the decked-out venue on the left and a simple farmhouse with a wraparound porch some four hundred yards ahead.

Once parked, he fell into step beside Harper, hand instinctively touching the small of her back. She started and looked at him with inquisitive eyes that gave no indication as to whether she welcomed the touch.

Not that he'd intended to cross whatever invisible boundaries they'd placed between themselves. It was just that being here, in this place with Harper, felt all too familiar. So familiar, his body seemed to be reacting to her presence as he had so easily before.

Except, things had changed.

But that didn't mean they couldn't change things back. Maybe tonight could be their first step in that direction.

She paused to gaze up at the entrance, swathed with cream and sheer curtains, white potted flowers on each side of the frame. "Beautiful."

He followed her line of sight to the barn's interior, lit by strings of lights encircling and draping from the rafters.

White linens covered long rectangular tables lined end to end, side to side, with walking space between. Every three or so place settings stood trios of glass vases of varying heights, banded with silver, matching cloth napkins placed on the plates.

Seeing the decorations, which were much fancier than he'd expected, he worried he'd told her to underdress. But while a few of the ladies were blitzed out, most of them wore outfits similar to Harper's.

Although none of them looked nearly as beautiful.

She'd always been unrivaled in that area. That was the main reason so many of the girls in their social circle had acted so ugly to her. They'd been jealous and afraid she might grow tired of CJ and try to steal their boyfriends.

She glanced about. "I'm guessing your parents want you to hobnob?"

He groaned. "I hope not, because I am so not that guy."

She laughed. "I remember the year you were voted homecoming king and everyone tried to pressure you into giving a speech."

"Only because they knew how much I'd hate it."

"I also seem to remember that you used me as your excuse not to."

"I truly was a little worried. I hadn't seen you for some time."

"I'm still upset with Maya Ward for telling you I was, and I quote, 'hiding in the bathroom.'"

"I'm sorry you felt you had to. If I'd known Sally Jo and her annoying echo were being so ugly, I would've done something."

"And made things worse. Besides, they got what was coming to them when someone found, copied and distributed the notes they'd been sending one another."

He chuckled. "Wow. I'd completely forgotten about that. Those were some of the most hilarious pages I've ever read."

He glanced toward a flash of red in his peripheral vision. *Perfect.* It was Sally Jo, the drama queen herself and, unfortunately, she hadn't grown up much since their teenage days. Based on the gossip folks attributed to her, the woman's contempt for Harper hadn't chilled much, either.

He touched Harper's elbow, her skin as soft as her strands of hair he used to run his fingers through. "Hate to say it, but look who decided to make an appearance."

She followed his line of sight. "And based on how tight, short and revealing her sequined dress is, hoping to snag herself a man."

"Guess some things never change."

"Seems not."

"I hope she won't make you feel uncomfortable."

That was the opposite of what he wanted. He was hoping this evening could be a big step toward winning back Harper's heart.

Before she and her adorable daughter returned to Seattle, potentially never to return.

Harper scoffed. "I seriously couldn't care less what that woman and her childish posse think of me, or say about me, for that matter."

So she'd heard the rumors. That had to sting, although her response indicated she took them for what they were—nothing more than the immature antics of people who'd peaked at sixteen and had yet to enter the world of adult decency.

"I would, however, love to try one of those." She pointed to an appetizer someone walking by was eating. It looked like a bite of steak wrapped in bacon.

"Let's get some." He led the way to one of numerous high-tops laden with veggie platters, hush puppies, some kind of cheesy pastry and numerous other items. "If this is what they call refreshments, I can't wait to see what they serve for dinner."

At the drink station, they ran into a woman Harper had interacted with at the mother-baby class she'd taken that morning. The two seemed engaged in a humorous conversation.

This was good. Every relationship she formed would make it harder for her to leave Sage Creek.

And him.

He was about to excuse himself when the ladies started talking about some ribbon acrobatics.

But then the band started playing one of Harper's favorite songs.

She turned to him with a grin. "Join us." She tugged him toward the dance floor, where a group of people, almost all female, were forming a line.

CJ resisted and shook his head. "I'm not really into those line dance deals. I'd just stumble all over the place and end up hurting a person."

"Or your ego?" She quirked a brow at him. "Seriously, it's the electric slide. No one could grow up in Texas without knowing how to do that one."

"Apparently, someone could have." He pointed at himself.

"I don't believe you."

"It's the truth. When y'all go left, I go right, and when you slide, toe-tap right, I fall backward."

"That's not how I remember things."

He swallowed as an image rushed to his mind from homecoming night. A slow song had come on that had reminded him of her. Something about a strong-willed, smart-witted woman who wasn't afraid to do things her own way, even if that meant going it alone.

At first, she'd been stiff in his arms, her gaze darting from him to the others swaying around them. But then he'd leaned close enough that his lips had brushed her ear and said, "I could've written these lyrics about you. If I could write, I mean."

She'd laughed, then locked hopeful eyes on his and asked, "You mean it?"

He'd nodded and spent the rest of the dance singing to her words she'd come to live out. A woman so unafraid to live independently, she'd left him behind.

But now Harper was back and asking him to dance in a space similar to the one in which they'd first begun to fall in love. He could keep resisting and spend the evening sitting bored at a table, wondering what might have happened had he said yes. Or he could embrace the moment.

And if doing so led to another heartbreak?

He needed to stop overthinking everything.

He turned back to Harper. "It's been a long time since I've done any kind of line dancing. Pretty sure I forget when to step where."

"I'll teach you." Her grin widened, and she

looked so incredibly beautiful, so happy, he couldn't disappoint her.

He laughed and fell beside her at the end of the line. "Don't say I didn't warn you."

"Slide, close, slide, tap."

He did his best to follow as she spoke out each step.

"Great job. When you go forward, swing your arm like this." She demonstrated.

He soon caught the rhythm and his moves felt more natural. While his steps weren't nearly as smooth as hers or her friend's, he no longer felt like he was about to stomp on somebody.

Then a slow song came on, and the crowd started to thin.

He took her hand. "You up for one more?"

Harper studied him a moment, her breath heavy and her cheeks red.

She bit her lip as if sensing the weight of this moment, same as him. "Okay."

CJ's heart gave a lurch as he pulled her to him, his hands resting on the small of her back as hers landed softly on his shoulders. Her eyes locked on his, her face so close, he could feel the warmth of her breath. Feeling her relax in his embrace, he leaned closer, inhaling the coconut-pineapple scent of her shampoo, and began to sing with the lyrics.

Just as he had when holding her, just like this,

on a dance floor many years prior—feeling again as if he could've penned the words for her. "'The first time I saw you, hair wild, eyes blue, you took my breath away. I fell in love that day.'"

"CJ." She pulled back to look into his eyes, a hint of uncertainty in her expression.

"Don't overthink this, Harper." He told her the same thing he'd been telling himself since they'd entered this space. Because, for now, he just wanted to enjoy the moment, knowing that it could easily be the last time he held her this close.

Did she feel the same? He couldn't be certain, but she once again relaxed against him, this time with her cheek on his chest, her face turned into his neck. Her breath tickled his skin, sending goose bumps up his arm.

He could've stayed like that for the rest of the night—feeling her soft warmth as the past and present merged in his mind and the dreams they'd once formed together reignited. He was in a dangerous place. He knew that. But he didn't have the strength to leave.

But then the tempo picked up, and the floor became crowded once again, and the moment was broken. When everyone started doing the Cotton Eye Joe, he slid out of the throng to an open chair at a nearby table. By then, Harper had gotten caught up helping two older women learn the complicated dance steps.

CJ couldn't keep his eyes off her. The way her face lit up when she laughed. Her wavy hair, shimmering beneath the lights above her, bouncing on her slender shoulders. How she noticed those who lingered on the edge, inhibited, and gently drew them in. Or came alongside those struggling to keep up.

Harper dominated the dance floor, only not in an obnoxious look-at-me kind of way. The music made her come alive with a joy that was contagious.

He'd always known this was her thing.

What did that mean for the two of them? Could she find what made her heart sing in Sage Creek?

If not, could he let her go a second time?

"I wondered how long it'd take her to get her hooks in you."

CJ turned to see Paul, the guy Harper had dated prior to him, standing beside him. He wore a charcoal-gray cowboy hat that looked fresh out of the box, and a plaid shirt with pearl buttons. A green-and-blue tattoo of a howling wolf stretched from his wrist to his elbow.

Shaking his head, Paul sat in the recently vacated chair to CJ's right. "Don't blame her none. I mean, a mama's got to do what a mama's got to do, right? Not surprised she'd target you, either."

He tensed. "What're you talking about?"

"You haven't figured it out yet? That ex-girl-friend of yours is hunting for a baby daddy."

CJ sat upright. "Dude. It's been…what, ten years? And you haven't gotten over her yet?"

"Oh, I'm long over that one, believe me. You, on the other hand." He shook his head. "Just can't let that one go, no matter how clear the lettering is on the wall. You realize she's playing you, right? That's what she does."

"You know nothing about her."

"And you do? History says otherwise, my man. If memory serves, you were about the last person to learn about her grand Seattle University Dance plans."

Jaw tight, CJ stood before he said or did anything he'd regret.

"Truth hurts, huh, Jenkins."

That guy didn't have a clue. Harper may have blindsided him that night, and completely broken his heart, but she'd never manipulated or used him. That had never been her way.

And if her time in the city and with that fancy dance company had changed her?

No. He refused to believe that.

Chapter Eleven

Nancy met Harper in the break room when she arrived at work Monday morning to ask if she wanted the weekend off.

Harper picked at her pinkie nail. "I really want to support CJ." The gleam in Nancy's eye suggested this response pleased her. "But I also need the money."

Nancy tapped a finger to her chin. "Let me talk with Ken."

She darted out and returned a moment later with a grin. "You up for pulling a double today and tomorrow?"

Harper mentally reviewed her library schedule. With their latest children's program ended and a brief lull before they launched the next, she wasn't due there until Wednesday afternoon.

"I need to check with my mom to make sure she can watch Emaline." Her response would show just how important this "girls' weekend," as she'd called it, was to her. It was one thing to suggest an idea—her mom was great at coming up with grand plans. Follow-through was another matter entirely.

"How about you give her a call? And if your mom's busy, you can always bring the pumpkin in."

"Are you sure?"

Nancy shrugged. "Don't see why not. I practically raised CJ here. As long as you don't go trying to lift eighty-pound cement bags off the shelves—which you shouldn't be doing anyway." She gave her a stern gaze.

"No, ma'am." Harper smiled, enjoying the renewed sense of camaraderie she'd started to experience with CJ's mom. They'd once been close.

She'd filled numerous maternal holes during Harper's teen years. Taught her to cook and bake, to treat others with kindness and respect and to expect them to do the same. But most importantly, whereas her mother often made her feel tolerated, Nancy had always acted as if the time spent with Harper had been the best part of her day.

After lunch, she found Nancy talking with CJ in her office.

She poked her head inside. "Hi. I spoke with my mom."

Nancy swiveled her chair to face her more directly. "And?"

"She's good to watch Emaline for however long I need."

"Yes!" CJ shot a fist in the air, making her laugh.

Nancy seemed equally pleased, making Harper more alert to the impact of her actions. CJ hadn't been the only one hurt when she'd left the last time, nor would he be the only one affected when it came time for her to move once again.

Maybe she shouldn't go to San Angelo after all.

But how could she decline, now that every plausible obstacle had been removed?

Besides, she was really looking forward to connecting with her mom. It'd be their first ever vacation together, unless you counted the time they drove, nonstop, to Cincinnati, Ohio, to take care of her grandmother recovering from knee surgery. They'd made the trip there in one day, barely left the house their entire time there, and Harper had been battling an intense stomach virus on the drive back.

As to watching CJ do his thing—Harper was simply going to show her support, like he had done for her countless times.

And she would do so while keeping her rogue emotions in check, a steadily decreasing skill, it seemed. It didn't help that CJ had started looking at her the same way he had not that long ago. But neither of them needed to repeat their breakup from five years prior. His pained expression the day she'd ended things had haunted her dreams for months.

Yet, despite the ache of knowing how deeply she'd hurt him, and her grief over the loss itself, she knew she'd made the right decision. Had she stayed, she would've always wondered whether or not she could succeed in the dance industry.

And if he'd tried to talk her out of going, or offered to join her?

Regardless, he hadn't. She'd chosen dance; he'd chosen the store. Neither of them chose each other. Seemed that meant something.

Over the next couple days, Harper tried to be exceptionally helpful, in part to thank Nancy for all the kindness she'd displayed, but also to keep herself from overanalyzing things between her and CJ.

The night before the event, she tossed and turned over her feelings for CJ and her difficulty shutting them down. She awoke with purplish bags under her bloodshot eyes and hair that refused to cooperate.

CJ stopped by before heading out, to offer her a ride. She felt a strong urge to accept but, thankfully, her brain stepped up before her mouth.

Standing at her open door, she glanced from

his truck and trailer filled with his tools and carvings to the pile of luggage behind her—admittedly more than they needed for a three-day trip. This was technically a mother-daughter-granddaughter trip.

She turned back to CJ. "I should probably ride with my mom, this technically being a girls' trip and all."

"Right." His smile faltered momentarily. He pulled his phone from his back pocket and glanced at the screen. "You ever try roulade?"

"Is that a game?"

He shook his head. "Melt in your mouth German beef pastry."

Odd question. "Can't say that I have."

"There's a restaurant in Fredericksburg that serves it. We could stop. It's on our way."

"San Angelo's only a few hours' drive, right?"

Again, his face fell. "Yeah."

She seemed to be shooting down all his ideas, not exactly a bad thing, considering they needed to spend less time together, not more.

Yet she found herself scrambling to reverse her words. "But I'm sure Emaline could use a midway break from her car seat." That was true. Her daughter tended to get bored and fussy after about forty-five minutes.

Her mom's patience for Harper's attempts to keep the baby entertained didn't last much longer.

He shot her the boyish grin that used to turn her insides to mush, and maybe still did. "Great. I'll text you the location."

She thanked him then stepped back inside, hand lingering on the doorknob.

"Don't know why y'all keep playing games with one another."

She turned to find her mom standing behind her with a burned piece of toast in one hand and a steaming mug of coffee in the other. Beyond her, Emaline bounced and chattered in her door jumper, thankfully wearing herself out some.

Harper frowned. "What are you talking about?" She picked up her packed duffel and Emaline's diaper bag, draping each from a shoulder.

"Don't act coy. I've seen how googly-eyed y'all are for each other."

Harper opened her mouth to respond, but her mom raised a hand.

"I ain't judging you none. Far from it. Dumbest move you made was letting that boy go." She took a bite of her toast, crumbs cascading from her mouth. "But I'll tell you this—you're going to lose him, for good this time, if you don't stop toying with his emotions. Then where will you be? I'll tell you where. In a pool of regret so big, it'll take a lifetime to climb out of."

Harper winced as fear pinged deep inside her. What if her mom was right?

Then again, she didn't exactly have a wealth of positive relationship experience to draw from.

Not wanting to say anything that might unleash more of her mother's sage advice, Harper squared her shoulders and once again opened the front door. "I'll load up the car."

Fastening her seat belt ten minutes later, she mentally prepared herself for more of her mother's lessons. Thankfully, her mom immediately started to sing to eighties' rock instead.

By the time they pulled into the Old German Bakery and Restaurant in Fredericksburg, the tension she'd entered her mom's vehicle with had turned to laughter. Lunch was pleasant and, thankfully, minimally awkward, even with her mother's not-so-veiled "What are your intentions with my daughter?" questions.

The remaining drive to San Angelo was uneventful.

Once they arrived, Harper smoothed a hand over Emaline's soft head. "I'd suggest we do some sightseeing before the contest starts, but if this peanut doesn't nap soon, she's bound to throw a fit." That wouldn't help CJ mentally prepare for his competition.

"I still can't believe she didn't fall asleep on the drive." Harper's mom handed her a spare hotel key. "Tell you what. Once we get all of our stuff to the room, why don't you leave the peanut with

Grandma and go help CJ get checked in to the contest and whatnot?"

"You sure?"

"Yep." She eyed CJ, who stood at the counter, getting his room, which, from the sounds of it, was right next door to theirs. "She and I will grab a quick nap then mosey around to see if we can't scope out the lumberjack scene."

Harper rolled her eyes. "You're insufferable. Please tell me that wasn't why you were so excited to come to this event." She hated to think that way, but her mom had once joined her for one of CJ's football banquets to flirt with his coach.

"Don't be ridiculous." She gave the back of Emaline's ruffle-hem blouse a tug. "But I'm certainly not going to waste this experience."

Harper couldn't shake the sense that she shouldn't, either. It was obvious, with how CJ kept jingling the change in his pocket, how much hope he was putting into the next three days. This contest could easily launch him as an artist, which meant that this weekend could be the most important of his life so far.

She'd get to share that moment with him.

As to the countless moments after, and knowing that should he reach his dream, it practically guaranteed he wouldn't follow her as she chased after hers?

She wouldn't think about that now. There'd be time for hard goodbyes later.

This weekend, she planned to show the most handsome, talented and honorable man in Texas the same support he'd showed her all those years ago.

CJ followed the map the hotel clerk gave him to San Angelo's vehicle-clogged downtown area then joined a line of half a dozen trucks and trailers similar to his waiting to drop their salable items at the consignment store.

He drummed his fingers on his steering wheel, trying not to fret about the competition. "Guess we're going to be here awhile."

"I'm in no hurry." She watched a potbellied man wearing large sunglasses and an American flag bandana around his head pulling a rolling cooler with one hand, holding a dog leash in the other, with two folding lawn chairs sandwiched between his arm and ribs. She turned back to CJ. "You nervous?"

He gave a slight shrug. "I've never worked in front of an audience—or been filmed—before."

"You'll do great. I have no doubt." She shot him a smile he felt all the way to his toes. "And like you said before, regardless how you place, this type of publicity will definitely put your name, and our town, on the map. Holy cow, can you imagine what the hardware store will be like come Monday morning? With folks clamoring in to see the new celebrity. It'll be like high school football all over again."

He laughed and placed his hand over hers. "Thanks for your support. This means a lot."

"Of course. Although you do know what'll happen if—*when*—you win, right, and get the money you need to buy that building with your friend?"

"What?"

"I'll be stuck at the hardware store with my biggest fan." The sarcasm was thick.

"Ken doesn't have anything against you. He can just be gruff at times."

Although, she was right about one thing. If CJ walked away with that prize check, his time at Nuts, Bolts and Boards, and therefore, with Harper, would be drastically reduced.

When they were just beginning to rebuild things.

What if the affection that had started to re-form between them dwindled with less time spent together and she once again decided to leave?

Did he really believe she could leave the dance world behind? They both knew she'd only returned out of necessity, which meant she could leave just as quickly.

Unless he gave her reason to stay.

"Hey, now." She gave him a playful shove. "Don't get so knotted up inside that you forget to have fun."

He shot her a grin. "Don't plan on it." That was, in fact, the last thing he planned to do—especially since this could be his best shot of winning her heart.

Once he and Harper, with the help of contest staff, got his consignment items loaded into their store and he'd signed all the necessary forms, they checked out the carvings by the other competitors.

He paused in front of a large stump with raccoons peeking between the thick, knobbed-off branches. "Some of these are really phenomenal."

"As are yours." She placed her hand, her skin warm and soft, in the crook of his elbow. "Besides, for all you know, this one could've taken decades. Whoever made it might not even be in the master competition."

"Not helpful."

She bit her bottom lip. "Sorry. What I—"

He smiled. "I know what you meant, and I appreciate it."

"I'm really proud of you for going after your dreams like this."

"Thank you." He probably should've said the same to her, the night she'd told him about her college plans. But in that moment, all he could think of was how her decision had affected him.

Did that make him less of a person?

The bigger question was how would he act if he found himself in that situation again?

He cast her a sideways glance. "You thirsty? Because I'm pretty sure someone just walked by with frozen lemonade."

"Let's go."

They strolled toward a long line of pop-up tents housing food and craft vendors. Numerous scents and noises swirled all around them. Hot dogs, funnel cakes, sunscreen. Laughter, people talking, music from two different directions. One came from a passing bicyclist who, apparently, had yet to discover headphones—and quality tunes. Another came from a local radio station that had sent hosts to cover the event.

Their van, black with their logo painted in thick, red lettering, stood behind a matching pop-up tent with two speakers anchored on either end. A man in plaid and a tan cowboy hat sat behind a table holding window clings, bumper stickers and other paraphernalia.

CJ cast Harper a sideways glance. If he grabbed her hand, would she pull away?

She paused at one of half a dozen tool companies' booths to look at an electric power cap. "What's this for?"

"To keep dust and whatnot from your lungs and eyes. It's got a fan that sucks in air from the top and filters out wood chips. Plus, it's air-conditioned."

"Seriously?"

"So I've heard."

"You don't have one?"

"I wish. Maybe once I start bringing in some green. These little jewels cost a pretty penny." He turned it over so she could see the price on the bottom.

"Wow. Although I'm guessing the other tools don't come cheap, either."

"Not exactly, but at least I can justify buying them for other things. A man always needs a good chain saw and grinder."

She laughed and moved on to a display of handcrafted jewelry. She picked up a teal-and-peach pair of earrings made from wood and resin. "My mom would love these."

"How'd the drive over go?"

"Better than I'd expected." She fingered wooden beads on a necklace. "I worried about how she and I would get along, with me living under her roof again. I know I annoy her sometimes. But I can also tell that she likes spending time with her first grandchild. And it's good for Emaline. I like that she's had so much one-on-one attention."

It was nice to hear Harper talk this way regarding her time in Sage Creek. Hopefully, all these positive experiences would motivate her to stay put.

They continued past a man selling customized charcuterie boards, another display of handcrafted jewelry and an older couple offering samples of homemade honeys and jams.

Harper eyed an opened jar of mint jalapeño jelly. "Interesting."

The vendor standing behind the table lifted a cup of pretzel sticks. "Would you like to sample some?"

Harper held out her hand. "No, thank you." She walked beside CJ as they continued on. "My dad used to love strange combinations like that. Popcorn and ketchup. Tortilla chips and peanut butter. Fries dipped in a chocolate milkshake."

"That last one I could do."

She scrunched her nose. "Remind me never to let you cook for me."

"Except, I already have. And if memory serves, you liked it."

She laughed. "I have to admit, you grill a mean steak."

"Your father. You talk to him much?"

She frowned and dropped her gaze. "I try. But he's never been that interested in me."

"I'm sorry." He remembered how much that had hurt her. She'd once told him that she knew in her head that he'd left her mom and that his abandonment wasn't about her. But that it was hard to believe that when he'd so easily walked away from her as well.

"I called him the day I got hired on with that touring dance company, so certain he'd be proud of me. Caught him while he was at a bar. I could hear how noisy it was on his end. Only, instead of stepping outside for even five minutes, he said it was too loud for him to hear me and could he call me back later."

"Did he?"

"Of course not. Probably forgot about it, and me, as soon as he hung up."

"I'm sorry," he repeated, not knowing what else to say. "Does he know about Emaline?"

"Yeah, and that I'm back home living with Mom." She snorted. "Doubt that surprised him any. He always said I was just like her."

Now CJ understood why that statement had hurt her so deeply. Most likely, her dad hadn't meant it in the way she'd taken it. Although, he might have. He'd never been high on the nurturing side. But that must've been how she'd made sense of his rejection. Her father hadn't walked away from her, as much as the part of her that resembled her mother.

He took Harper's hand and studied her expression, so much making sense. "Is that why you tried so hard not to be like her?"

"It's more complicated than that."

"Okay?"

"If you're asking why I moved to Seattle—" She shook her head. "Dancing is who I am."

"You're so much more than that."

"I get what you're saying. And obviously things didn't work out as I'd hoped. I know I need to course correct. It's just... I've spent years—hours upon hours—training. I don't want my hard work to be for nothing."

They'd stopped in the middle of the walking path, the jostle of people pushing past them alerting him to the fact that they were blocking traffic.

He pulled her aside and turned her to face him. He searched her eyes, struggling to speak. "You know I never asked you not to dance." His words came out as a hoarse whisper. "I just asked you to stay."

"Essentially, to give up my dream for you."

"It wasn't like that."

Tears brimmed in her eyes. "But it was. And we both know, if the shoe were on the other foot, you would've done the same."

"That's not true."

"Really?" Her tone held bite. "If you win this contest and someone offers you a shiny deal in New York or somewhere, you seriously believe you'd turn them down? For me? I mean, sure, I get that you can carve in Sage Creek. But you get my point. Do you really think, if forced, that you'd choose me over carving?"

"I would."

"Then why didn't you five years ago?"

"You never let me." His chest squeezed. "By the time I could breathe again, you were gone."

"You still could have come after me."

He dragged a hand across his jaw, frustrated with how their conversation had turned, and terrified one wrong word would shatter their relationship for good. "How would that have worked? I was a broke kid whose only job experience involved working for his parents."

That, according to Harper's friend, had been precisely what she'd said about him, and that was the reason he'd let her go. Because he'd believed he wasn't good enough for her. That she deserved, and would find, someone better than a pickup-driving, country-music-listening guy from the sticks.

"Besides," he said, "you'd made it clear you didn't want me."

"I don't want to talk about the past anymore." She gave his hand a squeeze. "We were nothing but a couple of stupid kids thinking we were ready to be grown. Which, obviously, we weren't." She started walking once again.

He sensed there was something deeper going on.

As they merged back onto the crowded sidewalk, he fell into step beside her.

Then it hit him. "You wanted me to fight for you. Because your dad never did."

Her steps halted as her gaze shot to him, the vulnerability in her eyes giving her an almost childlike appearance.

Chapter Twelve

The next morning, Harper hurried to get ready, not wanting to miss any of CJ's big day. Running her fingers through her still-damp hair, she glanced through the mirror to Emaline. She was sitting in her playpen, babbling and batting at a glittery spinning drum raised on a wooden stand.

Harper smiled and grabbed her mascara wand. "You making music, sweet girl?"

She squealed, and Harper laughed. "You carry a key about as well as CJ does, little one." Her heart warmed as she thought back to the evening she'd caught him singing that army theme song to Emaline in his kitchen. Such a sap.

Then she frowned, remembering their spat from the day before—if you could call it that, which she didn't. They'd simply…been rehashing junk they needed to let lie. Correction. She'd been rehashing things, and on the day of his big competition.

Some support she was.

Lord, help him to do well today. To think and carve quickly. Without losing any fingers.

The judges had given him and the others their challenge the night before. They had one day to carve out a sculpture that in some way symbolized passing time. Sunday, they'd receive scores for creativity, skill and artistic ability.

Her mom sat on the edge of the hotel bed, eating a bowl of dry cereal. "I was impressed with how quickly CJ landed on an idea last night. Guess all that brainstorming practice the two of you did gave him a head start on the competition, huh?"

"I hope so." Whereas some of the others had spent nearly half of their allotted "sketching" time staring at a blank page, or starting one idea then shifting to another, CJ had gotten straight to drawing. "He said the hardest part was balancing complexity with speed. Said a plan was only as great as its final execution."

"I s'pect so. You get a chance to talk to him once they finished for the night?"

She nodded. "Thanks for bringing Emaline back to the room."

Her mom shrugged. "I was ready to head back anyway. Can do the same tonight, if you'd like."

"I appreciate it." She turned around to face her. "Really. You've been great."

"Figure I wasn't always there for you like I should've been when you were growing up. Grateful for the chance of a do-over."

Tears stung Harper's eyes as the words she hadn't known she'd so desperately needed to hear washed over her. "Thank you for saying that."

Her mom nodded then stood and tossed her empty paper bowl in the trash. "Guess I best jump in the shower."

Harper was still processing her words, and CJ's from the night before, when she arrived at the contest site twenty minutes later. A steady hum and the spicy-sweet scent of cedar shavings filled the air.

The television crew was back with two cameramen, each shooting from different angles, and the crowd of spectators had nearly doubled. She worried both would only add to CJ's nervousness. If they did, he didn't show it.

She tried to make out his design from the blocked shape. He'd refused to tell her last night. Said he wanted to keep it a secret. She could tell how much he wanted to impress her, and that touched her.

Lifting Emaline from her stroller, she surveyed the competition arena, a large circular space encased by thick, five-foot logs standing on end side by side. The ground within was nearly covered with sawdust, with larger mounds accumulated beneath each carver's project secured on top of wooden pallets. Numerous electric cords snaked from somewhere outside the marked area.

A nasally voiced man behind her gave constant commentary on each of the competitors, loudly proclaiming their "obvious" errors and risky moves. "That kid's got guts," he said, clearly indicating CJ, the youngest of the group. "The guys he's up against have probably been carving about as long as he's been alive."

Harper resisted the urge to turn around and fire off a retort. So what that CJ was relatively new to all this? Whatever he lacked in experience, he more than made up for in creativity, of that she was certain.

She'd hoped to catch his eye, to offer him an encouraging smile, but he'd remained focused on his project from the time she'd arrived through now. The only brief pauses she'd seen him take had been for a swig of water or to switch tools.

To think, this weekend could be his big break—the event that piqued the attention of some of this nation's most affluent and influential art collectors.

Harper remembered how it felt, knowing you stood on the cusp of a dream. The excitement, anxiety and giddy anticipation. The realization that you could soon see the fruit of countless hours of hard work and sacrifice.

She thought back to what he'd said the day before, about her not giving him a chance to choose her. Would he now?

Did she want him to?

She shifted her weight, gazing toward wispy clouds drifting across the horizon. Could she be happy in Sage Creek? Considering she still hadn't heard anything about that choreographer's job she'd been waiting on, she might have to be. She was beginning to think her ex's mom had been feeding her a line to make Harper go away. Either that, or she didn't have the power she claimed and the position had been filled by someone else.

Now what? The longer Harper stayed out of the dance world, the harder it would be to break back in.

Could she find a way to do what made her soul sing in the town she was beginning to grow fond of—if it meant experiencing the type of love CJ had once promised her?

When the contest officiator signaled it was time to break for lunch, CJ set down the smaller chain saw he'd been using and shucked off his protective gear. He glanced up, his gaze sweeping the crowd. Upon seeing her, he grinned and headed her direction.

A few spectators, one a chubby kid with thick glasses and jet-black hair, another an older lady wearing a floppy green hat, intercepted him. Others stood nearby, waiting to catch a word, to ask a question, or maybe to congratulate him on his work.

She watched with a smile, amused to see he didn't seem any more comfortable being the center of attention now than he had back in high school.

His humility was one of his most endearing traits.

CJ caught her eye, and the look of exasperation displayed on his face was enough to motivate her to do the one thing every mom in the history of motherhood termed an atrocity—risk waking a sleeping baby. But then he slipped free and jogged toward her.

He released a heavy breath. "I thought I'd never break free."

"Guess it's tough being a celebrity, huh?"

"Yeah, right."

"You won't find that statement so absurd come Monday when everyone comes clamoring into the store to get their chain saws signed by the national carving champion."

"You think so, huh?" He glanced down at Emaline, tenderness radiating in his eyes. "Looks like someone's down for the count. She hot? Her cheeks look flushed."

"Probably just from all her fussing. I don't think she's thrilled that I'm making her wear noise-canceling headphones."

"Need to bring her back to the room?"

Harper bit her lip. She didn't want to miss the final segment of the competition. That's when CJ would most need her support, but she also worried Emaline could be becoming overstimulated. Most days, her world was rather quiet.

She shifted to extend her left leg, which was starting to cramp. "If she's still acting uncomfortable after her nap, I'll ask my mom to take her."

"You hungry?" He glanced at his phone then at the rows of booths stretching in either direction. "How about if I go grab us something to eat and a couple of iced lemonades?"

"I'm sorry. I meant to do that. I knew you wouldn't have much time for lunch, but then she fell asleep, and—"

"Hey, it's no big deal. I could use the movement, believe me."

"I can imagine." She reached for the diaper bag in the bottom of the nearby stroller. "Let me give—"

"Nope."

"At least let me—"

He'd jogged off before she could finish, and returned balancing a tray with three walking tacos, two drinks, chili fries and a large funnel cake.

She stared at it as he eased to the ground, nearly spilling it all. "Hungry much?"

He laughed. "Always." He poked a straw into one of the drink tops and handed it over. "Hope you don't mind, but I got us watermelon slushies. Just couldn't brave the line for the frozen lemonades."

"That bad?"

"You have no idea."

They ate in comfortable silence awhile, him gazing toward the contest arena, probably planning out his remaining hours, while she eavesdropped on conversations drifting by. A teenage boy was furious his parents wouldn't buy him a chain saw for his birthday and didn't think it fair that they held some "skateboard fiasco" against him. A group of men, dressed in nearly identical muscle shirts, was cracking "dad jokes." A middle-aged couple was fighting over who contributed most to their credit card debt.

CJ took a long pull on his drink. "You ever think about opening your own dance studio in Sage Creek?"

"A studio, yes. As to Sage Creek, it's crossed my mind. I just don't think there'd be enough business to sustain it." Otherwise, someone else already would've opened one.

"Doesn't every mom sign their little girl up for ballet?"

"That might be overestimating things a bit. But even if that were true, most parents and children lose interest once the kids reach fourth or fifth grade. I feel, to support Emaline and myself, I'd need more business than that."

"So find a way to appeal to the adults."

"What do you mean?"

"I once saw this place, like a bar but without alcohol, that had fifties' dancing. Folks came in, took a lesson, then spent the rest of the night doing their thing."

"Interesting." She took a drink of her slushy and told him about the fitness classes the ladies had talked about when she'd taken Emaline to Little Tykes.

"That something you're interested in?"

"I wouldn't know how to get started."

"Seems for the ballerina-style one, all you need is a wooden floor, a long bar attached to the wall and a floor-to-ceiling mirror. That acrobatics deal might be trickier. You'll want a building with strong support beams in the ceiling. And a business license and permits and whatnot."

She watched a ladybug crawl up a nearby blade of grass. "That sounds complicated."

"I could help with the legal stuff, and probably most of the remodel, too. Got a friend who'd tackle whatever I couldn't for cheap. He'd make sure everything was done right. Safe for your customers."

"That sounds expensive, even if your friend offers a hugely discounted rate. Finding a building, remodeling the place…"

"Maybe you could find a building that wouldn't need much of an overhaul. Like the community theater or something. Pretty sure they've got a wooden stage."

This discussion created mixed emotions. On the one hand, CJ was expanding her thinking. Could she find a workable facility close enough to prove feasible, and at a location people would actually visit? Whereas people in Seattle thought nothing of a thirty-minute drive, Sage Creek folks tended to stay close to Main Street.

The contestants around them started to migrate toward the competition area.

CJ looked around, glanced at his phone, grabbed their lunch garbage and stood. "Guess I best get back to it." He popped a few of his knuckles, a nervous tell. "Got to make the last four hours count."

She struggled to stand with minimal jostling to Emaline, who'd been sleeping much more soundly than expected, considering the noisy environment.

She smiled and, holding her daughter to her

chest, cheek against her shoulder, gave CJ's hand a gentle squeeze. "You'll do great."

His gaze intensified as his eyes latched on to hers. "Thanks." Emaline stirred and made a few whimpering sounds. "Hey, there, cutie." He skimmed her cheek with his knuckles. Concern lines etched across his forehead. "She seems warm."

Harper frowned and pressed her wrist to Emaline's temple, then glanced at the cloud-streaked sky. "I'd hoped she'd do okay so long as we stayed in the shade."

"Think you should take her back to the hotel?"

Harper scraped her teeth over her bottom lip. "I hate to miss the last, and potentially most important, hours of your event. But she does seem to have a fever. Let me call my mom right quick."

She got Patricia's voice mail. She was probably in the movie theater. She'd mentioned that morning that she wanted to see something.

As much as she longed to support CJ, Harper had to do what was best for her daughter.

"You go." He gathered her things and returned them to the diaper bag, and the bag to the stroller basket. "Judging isn't until tomorrow anyway."

Hopefully, Emaline would feel better by then or her mom would be willing to stay with her in the hotel, at least for the awards ceremony.

She placed Emaline in her stroller then stood,

told CJ she'd be cheering for him from the room, then left to get her little one out of the sun. By the time she'd reached the room, the baby had started crying.

"You uncomfortable, sweet girl?" She texted her mom, asking her to buy ibuprofen for infants, then lifted her daughter from her stroller. Holding Emaline, she paced, gently bounced and repeatedly sang the chorus of a lullaby—all that came to mind.

As Emaline drifted off, Harper grabbed the television remote and inched onto the bed with her back against the headboard. She was halfway through a romantic comedy when her mom burst in carrying numerous bags. One was from a local drugstore. It looked like the others were filled with items purchased from event vendors.

Her mom rummaged around in one, pulled out a small box of medicine, dropped the rest of her items onto the ground and strode to the bed. "Poor little munchkin. Think she caught a virus?"

"A cold maybe. Thankfully, she doesn't seem to be having any breathing trouble or a tummy-ache."

"Could have an ear infection. You used to get those all the time." She dropped into the hotel chair. "How's CJ doing?"

"Great. His sculpture is really starting to take shape."

"Any hints as to what it's of?"

"He's still really tight-lipped about it, but it looks like someone kneeling, with their hands outstretched, holding something."

"Interesting."

She nodded. "I know he's worried about having enough time for all the detailed work he wants to do."

"I'm excited to see it once he's done."

"Me, too."

She smiled at the image of him bent over his project, brow furrowed like it always did when he focused on something, jaw muscle clenching and relaxing as he worked. Biceps flexing every time he lifted the chain saw.

Her mom laughed. "Seems someone's finally waking up to her second chance."

Harper's cheeks heated. "What're you talking about?"

"You love him, and you know it."

She shifted, her gaze following the paisley pattern of the comforter. "I told you, I'm not staying."

Patricia closed her eyes and pinched the bridge of her nose. "You cannot tell me you're going to mess things up. Again. Seems you would've gotten better sense after the first time." She shook her head. "If you think you're going to find a better man in Seattle, or whatever city you go chasing off to, I'm telling you now, you're fool-ing yourself."

"Maybe I will and maybe I won't. Regardless, at least I'll know I gave my dreams my best shot."

"Even if it means losing CJ?"

She scoffed. "If I stay, and abandon the one thing I was created to do, I'll lose him anyway. Just like what happened with you and Dad."

"What do you mean?"

"You left college for him and ended up re-senting him for it." They'd practically destroyed one another. Hearing them fighting, calling each other names and throwing stuff had given her a perpetual bellyache as a kid.

"Your father and I had a lot bigger issues than whether or not I completed my degree. And he wasn't the reason I didn't. The excuse maybe." Her mom stood, got herself a cup of water, then sat back down. "I was flunking anyway—for the second semester in a row. I had a ton of stu-dent debt, and didn't see the sense in racking on classes I'd never pass. I just wasn't the school type, you know?"

Harper stared at her, assumptions she'd held for years crashing against this new information and tumbling into a swirl of confusion.

Her mom gulped down her water then tossed the paper cup in a nearby trash. "When your dad told me about his 'high-paying' truck-driving position, it seemed like my way out. Probably the stupidest decision I could've made. We'd only been dating a few months. But we were young, I was desperate, and he was cute." She laughed. "Of course, our time together wasn't a total waste. He gave me you, didn't he?"

Harper grabbed the remote. "Want to watch a movie?"

"In other words, change of subject?"

She gave a slight laugh.

"All right. I hear you. But let me say one more thing. If a dream costs you those you love, it's too expensive."

Her shoulders tensed. "God wouldn't have given me this passion if He didn't want me to use it."

"We both know I'm not much into religion. Still, seems to me Jesus is big enough to give you both—this dream you're chasing and the man who obviously adores you. *And* your daughter. But God might not do things the way you think. Don't go closing doors just because they're opening in places you don't expect."

CJ spent the rest of the afternoon completely absorbed in his project—until the contest facilitator gave the one-hour warning. After that, it felt like a fight not to waste time looking at everyone else's carvings. Every glance, however quick, would cost him more than time. It'd make it even harder for him to get back into "the zone," as Harper called it.

The fact that his muscles were beyond tired wasn't helping. He'd intentionally worked on his endurance while preparing for this event. But clearly not enough.

This type of thinking wasn't helping.

Refocusing on his project, he imagined the larger hands were his father's, those he was supporting were CJ's as a child, and the sapling in the soil was the ash tree they'd planted together after he'd first rode his bicycle without training wheels and fallen. Some might find a wipe-out a strange occurrence to commemorate, but through that, CJ had learned a crucial lesson. Failure wasn't something to fear but rather to be viewed as a courageous step toward tomorrow's success.

Assuming you got back on the bike, of course.

The man next to him let out an angry yell and CJ turned to see one of the carved antlers had broken off and was lying on the ground. Poor guy must have leaned on it or something. Although he could glue it back on, it might be heavy enough that he'd need to drill in a dowel for extra support.

Releasing a breath, CJ grabbed his rotary tool, fine grinding bit inserted, and started working on the last details on his hands. He'd managed to finish all the fingernails except the right pinkie when the final horn blew.

"Tools down and step away." The man's booming voice was about as intimidating as his tall, thick frame and sharp scowl.

Some people in the crowd cheered. Others hooped and hollered, and someone bellowed, "Moose!"

CJ chuckled. Considering the only large animal he saw resembled an ibex, the guy must've been rooting for one of the carvers. He shucked off his protective gear and jiggled his T-shirt in an attempt to shake off the thick coating of sawdust. A hot shower would feel amazing.

The officiator turned toward the audience. "We invite you all to vote for your favorite carvings, using the QR codes posted at each. You may do so up until 9:00 a.m. tomorrow. The results will account for 25 percent of each contestant's score, which will then be factored in with the judges'. We will announce the winner tomorrow at 11:00 a.m."

Reading that in the contestant notes felt a lot less nerve-racking than hearing it relayed now, knowing he had a good eighteen hours to wait.

CJ scrubbed a hand over his face and shot Harper a text.

She responded immediately, as if she'd been waiting to hear from him. Send me a picture!

Her enthusiasm made him smile. I'd rather show you in person.

When she sent a sad face, he dialed her number.

"Hey." She sounded even more tired than he felt and, based on the way Emaline was wailing on the other end, he could understand why.

"Rough night?"

"How'd you guess? I really want to come down there, but I don't feel right about leaving."

"No, of course. Tomorrow. Will y'all be able to sleep tonight?"

"I feel like I should be asking you that same thing. You anxious?"

"Not enough to override my sheer exhaustion."

She laughed. "Get some rest."

"See you tomorrow."

This conversation reminded him of all the late-night phone calls they'd shared back in high school. Reluctantly saying good-night, knowing they'd reconnect the next day.

Lord, tell me I'm not foolish for feeling that way now. That things will end differently this time.

That they wouldn't end at all.

CJ still had the engagement ring he'd intended to give her. Over the years, he'd told himself he was simply making the wise financial choice by keeping it. After all, he'd worked and saved long and hard to buy that thing. The truth was, he'd not had the heart to part with it.

He'd been unable to acknowledge that before, for fear he was denying reality.

Now he was glad his heart hadn't given up hope.

Chapter Thirteen

Sunday morning, they arrived at the conference arena to find half of Texas, it felt like, milling about. People were talking about the various designs and accessing the QR codes with their phones.

CJ ran a hand over Emaline's head. "Peanut seems to be doing better. She sleep okay?"

"Once I got her down, yeah."

"And you?"

"Like a rock."

"Me, too."

Harper was surprised. She'd expected him to be wired with anticipation for today's results.

He acted casual and confident, but the way he kept adjusting his cowboy hat and jingling coins in his pocket revealed his anxiety level.

Halted behind a handful of slow-moving voters, she gave his hand a squeeze. Her heart skipped when his gaze, radiating obvious adoration, locked onto hers.

He was so incredibly handsome when his tenderness showed through. Good-looking anytime, but when his more sensitive side emerged especially.

She cleared her throat and shifted Emaline to her other hip.

"What do you think of all this, cutie?" CJ gave the baby's foot a gentle tug. "Would you cast your vote for mine?"

They inched forward, past a carving of various stages of the moon, each raised on a dolly, then one of a tombstone.

Harper regarded it with a raised eyebrow. "So cheery."

"And maybe a bit of inspiration to encourage folks to get to living. Pastor Roger always asks us what we plan to do with the dash between our birth and death dates. Not sure what all the Good Lord will have me do between now and then, but I do plan to excel in one area."

"Which is?"

"Learning to love well." The increased intensity in his eyes suggested he was talking about her.

Not sure what to say, she turned toward an old-fashioned church steeple with exposed brick peeking through peeling paint. Built, refurbished, and other dates were carved into the siding. "Other than various bouts of remodeling, what do you think this person was trying to convey?"

CJ angled his head. "Maybe all the special moments lived by individuals and families, going back for generations? Weddings, baptisms, first communions and end-of-life celebrations."

An image of Trinity Faith came to mind and the many faces she'd seen within its walls over the years. She'd formed numerous memories in the building, despite her limited time there growing up.

Although, that was changing. She'd made God a promise—if He gave her the hardware job, which He had, then she'd make her faith a bigger priority. She was doing her best to honor that, and had found that she actually enjoyed her Sunday mornings and had even started listening to a daily Bible podcast.

CJ stopped in front of a goatlike animal with large curved horns. "Although I still haven't figured out how this piece represents the passing of time, you've got to admit, the guy's got talent."

Feeling like acknowledgment would almost be a betrayal, Harper gave a slight nod. "It's interesting to compare everyone's ideas, for sure. But I'm most anxious to see what you chose to make." And through it, to catch a deeper glimpse of the man she was growing to love—again.

Maybe she'd never stopped.

The family of four in front of them veered left, allowing her to see CJ's final project.

"Here it is." He motioned to a carving of a man kneeling, cupped hands extended before him, cradling another pair of hands that held a sapling sprouting from a mound of dirt.

Harper's throat burned. The paternal image pricked the longing she held for Emaline to grow up with a loving father. A man like CJ, who clearly understood the impact of an attentive dad.

She stepped closer. "It's beautiful."

He grinned. "Yeah?"

She nodded. "Tell me about it."

He relayed a story about when he'd first been learning to ride a bike. "I was trying to act brave but, truth is, I would've been content to keep my training wheels on—indefinitely. Only, I wanted to make my dad proud. So, I hopped on and took off like a bullet, pedaling as fast as my five-year-old legs could go. Ended up eating concrete."

"Ouch."

He nodded. "Skinned my knees and hands pretty good. Might've cried a bit. Although I tried my best to fight it. I worried my dad would be disappointed in me. Was mighty confused when he ran up to me, clapping and praising me like I'd just finished the Tour de France."

She frowned. "No offense, but that sounds mean. Like he was celebrating your fall."

"No, but he was celebrating every pedal that led to it. But yeah, maybe my crash and burn, too, so that I wouldn't be devastated when my efforts didn't turn out as I'd hoped."

"He didn't want life's setbacks to paralyze you."

"Right. Which is why we planted that tree in our yard. As a daily reminder of a lesson he reiterated often when I was growing up."

"Your dad's a wise man."

He nodded. "A great role model." He looked at Emaline once again and tickled her under her chin. "Think you and I can plant something one day to celebrate your first wipeout, peanut?"

Harper's heart squeezed. CJ had just inserted himself into Emaline's future. It scared her to realize how much that meant to her. How much she wanted that for her daughter.

Was that what she wanted for herself? Now that it appeared that her choreographer's job wouldn't happen, she was rethinking a lot of things.

But how much of her feelings for CJ were entangled with her desire to give Emaline a father?

She didn't want a plan B romance.

As to the promises Emaline's paternal grandmother had made, she'd been half tempted to text her a snarky "Like mother, like son." Instead, she'd asked about the job, not expecting a response but wanting to demonstrate she wouldn't be easily brushed aside.

Why was she even fretting over that woman or anything she'd said? If she'd been a person of integrity, she never would've driven Harper away in the first place.

Maybe it was time Harper pursued child support. Or rather, past time. She wasn't thrilled with the idea of going to court, but it was something she needed to learn more about.

CJ's stomach rumbled loud enough for her to hear it above the conversations occurring around them.

She laughed. "Hungry?"

"Starved. Ate a bunch of snacks last night for dinner and skipped breakfast this morning." He looked at his phone screen. "Want to grab a bite?"

"Let me call my mom, but yeah." She pulled out her cell and clicked on her mom's contact.

"Hello?"

"Hey." She relayed CJ's question. "Want to join us?" Seemed right to ask, considering this was supposed to be a girls' weekend. While they'd spent a lot of time together in the hotel, they hadn't done much else.

"And be the third wheel?" Her mom scoffed. "No, thank you."

"It wouldn't be like that."

"Don't worry. I'm not offended. I'm thrilled. Like I told you before, it's about time y'all quit mousing about and admit you're in love."

"I'm not—" She clamped her mouth shut, her cheeks heating as her gaze shot to CJ. "If you're sure you don't want to come."

She ended the call, returned her phone to the diaper bag's side pocket, then turned to CJ. "Mind if we swing by the hotel for Emaline's stroller?" She'd left it in her room so she wouldn't have to push it through the crowd.

"No problem."

Hand to the small of her back, he led her through the steady stream of people on the sidewalk.

They chose a breakfast place that required a quick drive in his truck to get there. Harper had brought a portable cloth high-chair contraption she secured to a chair. She ordered an egg-white veggie omelet with a cup of fruit. He chose pancakes and bacon with two extra strips, then drenched his food in syrup.

She poured a cream packet into her coffee. "Still haven't lost your football player appetite, I see."

He laughed. "Guess fourteen hours of carving built up an appetite." He couldn't remember the last time his biceps and shoulder muscles had been this sore.

"I imagine. I used to be starving after dance rehearsals."

"Did you all have to watch what you ate?"

She regarded his plate with a raised eyebrow. "I didn't turn my breakfast into a sugary soup, if that's what you mean."

He chuckled. "Hey, now." He took a swig of water. "When you were with that touring company, did you have long days?" He felt torn between wanting to prolong this meal as long as possible and getting back to the competition site. Not that there was much point in that. He wouldn't know anything for a couple more hours.

"Sometimes, yeah. But you also learn to rest on your off days. Otherwise, an injury can take you out for an entire season."

She talked about a typical day from warm-ups, rehearsals and ongoing technical classes, along with some of the places she'd visited. "Once, we did a series of performances in Southern California. Most were back-to-back. But we did get a couple days off to visit the beach. By then, I was so exhausted, I pretty much slept."

Forking a chunk of pancake, he studied her. What he was about to ask could end their pleasant conversation right quick, but he needed to know. "Emaline's dad. He still in the picture?"

Harper stared into her coffee mug, slowly stirring with her spoon. "He's not interested." Her voice was soft, and he wondered what kind of wounds she'd experienced.

"You love him?"

She seemed to flinch. "What? No." Her expression hardened. "He was a jerk who preyed on all the new dancers and got away with it because his mom had pull in the dance world. Or at least made everyone believe she did."

"I'm sorry. That must be hard."

"Sometimes. It'd be nice to have a life partner to talk things through with."

He wanted to tell her he could be that, but not here. Not now. Once they got back to Sage Creek and he had the ring to propose to her proper, then he'd tell her everything—his feelings and his hopes. For all three of them.

After breakfast, they still had time to kill so they decided to meander through San Angelo's historic downtown area. They started at a women's boutique Harper deemed "adorable" with its handwritten chalkboard signs and shelves and displays made from dressers. Ambling down the brick sidewalk, they eventually reached the general store Harper's mom had told her so much about. After purchasing some trip mementos, they headed back.

Harper's mom was waiting for them when they returned to the contest arena.

"There's Nana's sweet muffin." She kissed Emaline's forehead then straightened. "Where y'all been? I was starting to get worried."

Harper relayed their morning.

"Sounds lovely." She turned to CJ and handed him a gift bag she'd been holding. "Here."

He wrinkled his brow. "What's this for?"

"To celebrate your win, goof."

"But they haven't announced that yet. I'm not even confident I'll place."

"Don't underestimate yourself, sugar. You've got as much of a shot as any of the others."

"I appreciate that, ma'am." Not the most encouraging praise he'd heard, but he appreciated the effort. "Talent aside, I've been rethinking their scoring. Seems locals might have a bit of an advantage."

Mrs. Moore angled her head with a frown and glanced around. "Oh. You mean they might've monkeyed with the results by calling in all their buddies and favors?"

He shrugged. "Can't say I'd blame them. If this contest were anywhere near Sage Creek, I'd probably be asking about everyone I knew to come cast votes for me."

"Good point. Harper told me about your and

your friend's plans for that building. What're you going to do if you lose?"

"Mom!" Harper's face flushed.

CJ laughed. "It's okay. That's a fair question. I expect the owner will have sold it by the time I save up my portion. Although, I'd rather see my friend find someone else to go in on it with." Hopefully, he'd still have time to do so, if need be.

"And then?" Mrs. Moore pulled a granola bar from her purse and tore open the package. "You going to go back to working for your parents?"

His gaze shot to Harper, the statement she'd told her friend back in high school, about him lacking ambition, stinging afresh. She'd seemed so proud of him for entering this contest and for carving in general, as if both had changed her previous opinion of him. Would his returning to Nuts and Bolts undo that?

Rubbing the back of his neck, he shifted his weight. "I'll keep plugging away and start looking for another place. Regardless, I *will* open my own business. Even if I have to eat beans and rice for the next couple years to save the cash to make it happen."

"I admire your drive." Harper's eyes radiated warmth.

He couldn't contain his grin. "Thank you."

"Anyway, hope you like the gift I got you." Patricia motioned to the bag. "I was in one of those souvenir stores yesterday. Figured I might as well get you something, just in case." She pulled Emaline from her stroller and, bouncing and swaying, told them about some gag items she'd found when a horn blew, indicating it was time for CJ and the others to stand by their carvings to await the final scores.

His stomach dipped. "Guess this is it."

Harper reached for his hand, gave a squeeze, and, for a moment, their eyes locked.

It felt like the next fifteen minutes dragged on as the officiator explained the scoring categories, specific things the judges were looking for and the cash awards given for the top three placers. Then the man read information each contestant had entered regarding how their carving conveyed the passing of time. CJ had overheard some people complaining about not knowing this prior to casting their votes. He sort of agreed, but he also understood the reasoning. For one, he and the others had only learned of the challenge Friday. Plus, the judges were also probably gauging how clearly the carvers conveyed their ideas to the public.

The man paused and made a visual sweep of the audience. "Y'all ready for the final results?"

Everyone cheered. A few people whistled and,

once again, a deep voice somewhere to the right started chanting, "Moose! Moose! Moose!"

The officiator motioned for everyone to quiet down. "In third place, with a score of eight-point-five out of ten, is *The Good Old Days* by Ron Bangle."

The tall, lanky man two projects over gave a whoop and strode forward, bent arms raised, hands fisted.

CJ eyed the wagon holding a ball, floppy baseball mitt and stuffed bear the man had created. He didn't know whether to feel encouraged or discouraged. On the one hand, there were still two open slots. But that also meant he'd need an eight-point-six at a minimum to place. That left little room for error. Not to mention, that man's use of nostalgia had probably grabbed a good number of the older generation's votes.

Jiggling the coins in his pocket, he released a tense breath. He looked at Harper, her big smile and thumbs-up sign motivating him to stand a bit taller.

If he was going to lose this thing, he'd at least look confident doing so.

"In second place…" The man's booming voice made CJ jump. Shifting from one foot to the next, he cracked his neck, first one way then the next.

"With a score of eight-point-nine out of ten,

we have *A Man's Legacy* by Christopher James Jenkins."

He blinked, not sure he'd heard right.

"CJ, that's you, boy!" Patricia's voice rose, almost shrill, above the cheering crowd.

He looked her way to see her waving her free arm like she was trying to flag down a plane or something. Beside her, Harper was jumping up and down, hands to her chest.

He froze, vision locked on her.

Man, did he love her. Seeing her response, and her expression of joy, made him believe that she loved him as well.

"Dude."

He turned toward the gravelly voice to his left. "You gonna go up, or what?"

CJ gave a nervous chuckle, his face hot and his heart so full, it felt ready to burst from his chest. "Oh, right."

Tipping his cowboy hat at the audience, he sauntered to the center of the arena for his trophy and accompanying check. Neither of which meant nearly as much as knowing he'd won Harper's heart.

Again.

This time, he intended to keep it.

He didn't hear much after that, or see much else, except Harper's smiling, sun-kissed face standing amid the crowd.

Once the event ended, he lingered in the arena, chatting with one of the other contestants to give the crowd time to thin out so he wouldn't be thronged by the more energetic and talkative spectators. He'd probably need to learn to deal with these types of situations if he wanted to become a successful carver. But all the attention was more than a little overwhelming.

His newfound friend adjusted his ball cap. "Best get home to the missus." The two shook hands. "If you're ever in the Branson area, make sure to give me a holler."

CJ nodded, knowing the guy was simply being friendly, and followed a few steps behind him.

The moment he stepped from the arena, Harper tackled him in a hug. "I knew you could do it!" She bounced with enough enthusiasm to jiggle his insides.

Relishing the feel of her soft frame pressed against him and the faint pineapple scent of her shampoo, he wrapped his arms around her, reluctant to let go.

"You realize he didn't win, right?"

He laughed at her mom's incredulous tone.

Harper gasped and pulled away.

Patricia looked at her. "What? Was that rude?"

Grinning, he twined his fingers in Harper's. "No offense taken, ma'am. And, yes, I do realize that."

Her mother smiled. "Oh, good. Well, then, how do you intend to celebrate?"

"By asking my friend Oliver to meet me at the Realtor's office so we can make an official offer."

"Yes!" Harper's eyes gleamed. "Can I see it? I mean…is that allowed? I know it's not yours yet."

He smiled. "I'd like that."

Chapter Fourteen

❧

CJ called Oliver on his way to settle up with the event consignment store. His friend said he wasn't surprised he'd placed, but his immediate "Yes!" suggested he'd been worried. That was understandable considering the deadline his landlord had given them to make him an offer on the building. Although the man had held off for Oliver's sake, the listing would go live in a few days.

"Nothing like cutting it close to the wire, huh?" CJ parked next to a yellow pickup with plastic taped across a busted window and got out. "I should be leaving here within the hour, which would put me back in Sage Creek by three thirty." Pocketing his keys, he strolled into the busy store.

He recognized a handful of customers from those he'd seen in the audience during the event and assumed that's where most of the others had come from as well. Although, it was fun to think that maybe the local television and radio stations had drawn people out.

"Mr. Jenkins." A woman wearing a brown-and-teal plaid dress that hit a foot above red cowgirl boots greeted him with a smile. "Congrats on receiving second place." Her name tag read Delilah.

He tipped his hat at her. "Thank you, ma'am." The recognition felt odd, but hopefully it had translated to increased sales. Had the spectators purchased much yet?

He glanced through the crowd, pleased to see that some of his items had sold. He was tempted to call Oliver back and suggest they meet later, or even the next day. But he wouldn't do that, not with how excited his friend had been.

Besides, he'd waited long enough.

"Please visit the back checkout counter to receive payment for whatever items you sold." Delilah motioned to a long, rustic counter set against the far wall.

"Appreciate it." He filed in line behind two other competitors. From the sounds of it, the first guy, a fella who hadn't placed, would be leaving with all his pieces and wasn't thrilled. Next up, the man who'd carved the church with exposed brick was walking away with a couple thousand.

When CJ stepped up to the counter, the man

behind it flashed him a smile. "Mr. Jenkins. Impressive work today."

"Thank you."

"You were a hit here as well. Sold just shy of half your pieces." He flipped through a stack of papers to his right and pulled out CJ's consignment form. "As you may know, we have a relationship with a local art gallery."

CJ stood a tad taller. "I read something about that on y'all's website."

"Then you may remember that, each year, their dealer selects a handful of carvings to sell in their showroom." He handed CJ a sheet of paper.

He read the terms. "Seventy-thirty split. Not bad. They want them all?"

"Yep."

CJ fought to contain his enthusiastic smile behind a casual smile. "That makes things easy." He took the check for the sold items, thanked the guy and sauntered out, his feet feeling light despite his fatigue from the stressful and physically exhausting weekend.

With nothing besides his tools and gear to load into his trailer, he made it to Sage Creek earlier than anticipated. Waiting in the Realtor's parking lot, he turned off his radio and looked at the clear blue sky. *Lord, I feel like You have flooded my life with blessings. The contest, the gallery, this business and Harper.*

His throat turned scratchy at the memory of her practically knocking him over with her enthusiastic hug, of how right she'd felt in his arms and the look in her eyes that suggested she felt the same.

God had returned to him the woman he loved. And that was a better gift than all the others CJ had received combined.

Now to make sure he didn't mess things up.

And if another dancing opportunity arose?

He'd simply figure out a way to hold tight to her. He refused to believe God would bring them back together just to take her away from him.

Three quick beeps on a horn alerted CJ to Oliver's arrival. Grinning, his friend pulled in beside him. They jumped out of their vehicles simultaneously and fell into step with one another as they proceeded up the flower-lined walk.

"Dude. Second place, cash money, and on television, all in the same weekend. What's next, a national tour and book deal?"

CJ laughed. "As long as they'd take a three-page pamphlet, sure."

"Want to grab a burger after this? To celebrate?"

"Rain check? I'm meeting Harper at the building to give her a look-see."

Oliver paused with his hand on the open door.

"Really? You two a thing again?" His tone carried a note of concern.

"I wouldn't say that." But they seemed to be heading that direction. He wanted to think she was feeling the same way.

"Hello." Gabrielle came from around the corner. "Come on back."

She led them to a small conference room with powder blue walls decorated with photographs bearing various inspirational quotes. Twenty minutes later, she was walking them out with a promise to call as soon as Oliver's landlord responded to their offer.

"I'm not worried." Oliver initiated a handshake.

CJ did the same, then followed him out and to their vehicles. "Hey, thanks for waiting for me on this."

"Never would've found anyone else foolish enough to share buildings with me."

They both knew that wasn't true.

CJ called Harper as he was leaving.

"That's so exciting." He could picture her radiant smile on the other end. "Text me the address and I'll meet you there. Mind if I bring Emaline?"

"I'd be bummed if you didn't."

She paused. "You're amazing, you know that?"

Warmth swept through him. "Just a mite smitten with that peanut." And her mother.

A shrill chirping sounded from her side. "Ugh! The cookies! I've got to go."

Smiling, he shook his head. Same old Harper. One thing was certain, he wouldn't be marrying her for her kitchen skills.

He *did* plan to marry her. He'd considered proposing to her while they were in San Angelo but worried he'd be too stressed with the contest to think straight, let alone say the words to sweep her off her feet.

Tonight was better, anyway. The perfect end to an amazing weekend, and a relationship he intended to continue investing in until his last breath.

After a quick stop at his house to pick up the engagement ring, he hurried to the building he and Oliver would soon own. The exterior wasn't much to look at now. More of a barnlike structure with an old-fashioned, covered wooden-plank walkway. But they'd get it spruced up soon enough.

When Harper pulled in, he stepped out of his truck and met her at her car. "Hey."

"Hey." She smiled, and his gaze fell to her soft, pink lips.

Lips he planned to kiss soon, assuming she said yes.

She had to. He wasn't sure his heart would recover otherwise.

He moved to the back passenger door. "Mind if I get the munchkin?"

"Not at all. I find it adorable how much you seem to enjoy her."

"Well, she does laugh at all my jokes."

"What jokes?"

"You just proved my point. Sheesh." He rolled his eyes with a grin. "Some people have no sense of humor." He gently tossed Emaline in the air then brought her to his face and nibbled her neck. Her happy squeals made him chuckle. "Come on, peanut. Let's see what I got myself into."

Ascending the sagging step he planned to fix first thing, he motioned with his head for Harper to follow.

The interior was dark and musty and smelled like his grandmother's attic. He flicked on a switch, and a series of light bulbs dangling from beams in the ceiling came on.

"This area belongs to Oliver." He indicated the space spanning the right half of the building and filled with everything from vintage jewelry to antique tools and toys. "This here will be mine." He led the way into the large, open area previously used as a secondhand clothing store.

Unfortunately, the previous tenants had left him a bit of a mess, but nothing he couldn't clean out in a couple of days.

She touched the deeply grooved wooden wall,

which matched the floor. "This will be perfect for you!"

"I think it'll fix up nice."

"You have an idea of what you want to do?" Her phone rang. She glanced at the screen, studied it for a moment. "Seattle area code." Her expression tightened. "Maybe I should take this. Sorry."

"Go ahead. Emaline and I will just be planning our renovation strategy, isn't that right, peanut?"

She laughed and, rotating slightly, took a sidestep. "Hello, Harper Moore here."

Her eyebrows shot up. "Yes, sir? How can I help you?" The lilt in her voice matched the smile gradually taking form on her face. "I completely understand." Her gaze shot to CJ and lingered, worry lines stretching across her forehead.

Was something wrong? His posture stiffened, his ears perked to her conversation.

"Absolutely. May I check my calendar and get back to you?" She paused and her expression brightened. "Wonderful. Thank you, Mr. Garcia."

She ended the call and turned to face him, her eyes searching his.

Her rapid change in demeanor left his gut unsettled. "Is everything all right?"

She rubbed at her hairline and nodded. "That was the managing director of a theater in Portland, Oregon."

"Okay." This couldn't be good. He wanted to end this conversation before she said more, but he knew that wouldn't change whatever would come next.

He wanted to trust that nothing she'd heard in that call would affect their relationship but, unfortunately, their history said otherwise.

Harper seemed to have difficulty maintaining eye contact as she told him about a promise made, and apparently kept, by Emaline's paternal grandmother.

"Is that what you want? To be a choreographer?" He struggled to get the words out.

"I don't know. But this opportunity..." She released a breath. "I need time to process."

"Fine." Throat tight, he kissed Emaline's temple and handed her over. "Let me know when you've got that figured out." Jaw clenched, he strode toward the door then stopped and turned back around. "I'll lock up behind you."

"CJ, please."

The pain in her eyes stabbed at his heart, but not enough to override the gaping wound reopened within him. He should've known this would happen. He had known, but had convinced himself, beyond common sense, that this time would be different.

That their reconnecting had been orchestrated by God.

She pressed her fingers against her collarbone. "Are you saying you want me to leave?"

"I think that would be best."

Harper needed time to think. Not wanting to sit in an empty house while Emaline napped, she chose to drive out into the country.

With Emaline happily cooing in the back seat, likely moments from falling asleep, Harper allowed her mind to drift as she focused on the scenery around her.

The vibrant roadside flowers and quiet pastures dotted with longhorns, centered by barns, many of them older than her, her mother and her baby combined, soothed her. Bordering the long, winding highway, the landscape emitted a calm, relaxed air that gave her space to untangle everything swirling through her brain and heart.

She loved CJ. She did. Even more than she had when they'd been teenagers. But could she pass up this opportunity that, if handled well, could lead to many more, for a life in Sage Creek, Texas? Or would she always wonder what might've happened, had she followed her dreams?

Yet, if she left the man she loved, who loved her and clearly loved Emaline as well, would she regret it?

She'd never find another CJ. She knew that.

Neither would she find a choreography position like the one Mr. Garcia was trying to fill.

A position that wasn't yet hers. She still had to interview, like everyone else, although he was willing to fly her out next week to do so. That sounded promising.

If only he'd called her a week, or even three days, ago, before San Angelo, the weekend during which CJ had captured the last reserved places in her heart.

Was the timing of his phone call, so quickly after she'd decided to search for a space to open her own dance studio, a sign that God was directing her differently? Or was the fact that the man had reached out *after* she'd finally opened her heart, fully, to remaining in Sage Creek a sign that she should stay?

Tears pricking her eyes, she gazed toward the purple hills stretching across the horizon.

Lord, I don't know what to do. I'm not so great at this listening for Your voice thing yet, or even knowing what that might sound like.

She thought back to what her mom had said about Jesus being big enough to give her both of her dreams—the man she loved and a fabulous dad for Emaline, and a life spent working in her dream career.

Her daughter's deep, rhythmic breathing behind her indicated she'd finally given up her fight to keep her eyes open. After all the excitement she'd experienced over the past couple of days, she'd probably be out for a good two hours.

That should give God plenty of time to speak.

Her gas tank, however, wouldn't allow for that long of a drive.

She pulled onto a long dirt road bordered by wind-stirred fields and cut the engine.

Closing her eyes, Harper leaned against the headrest, trying to tune in to the "still small voice," as Trisha often called it. But all she could hear were her own thoughts pinging rapidly through her brain.

At least, she was relatively certain most if not all of them came from her.

With a huff, she called Trisha.

"Harper. What's up?"

She gave a shortened version of what had happened.

"Oh, wow. Okay." Trisha paused. "Can you choreograph and teach dance from Sage Creek?"

"You mean open my own studio? I don't know. I've been thinking about it, only that takes a lot of money."

"What if you rented space from someone else?"

Harper relayed her concerns regarding sufficient business. "Although, I could maybe supplement through some sort of fitness class." She told her about her conversation with the ladies from the Little Tykes class.

"Oh! Yes! Little Tykes would be a great space, and that would probably help Julia out a lot."

"What do you mean?"

"I guess she's been struggling some. So much so that she's worried she'll have to shut down."

"That's sad." Harper knew what it was like to feel as if life trampled on your dreams.

"It is, but also potentially good for you in that she might be open to some sort of partnership. You should give her a call—before you make any big, potentially relationship-shattering decisions."

"Okay. That settled, now to the important question. Are you looking for an ice cream buddy tonight?"

She laughed. "Tempting." Was Trisha's mention of Julia God's leading? Or simply a potential idea offered by a friend? "Actually, I was wondering…how do you figure out what God wants you to do?"

"Well, a lot of ways, and I think He probably speaks to us all differently, but first, I pray."

"I did that."

"Yeah?" She sounded impressed. "Good for you."

"Now what?"

"I suggest you take some time to quiet yourself in His presence."

"What does that mean?"

"Ask Him to cleanse your heart of everything that isn't from Him, then take some time to simply praise Him for who He is."

"Like we do at church?"

"Exactly. Then close your eyes and wait."

"For how long?"

It was Trisha's turn to laugh. "That, my friend, is the thousand-dollar question, to which I would say, it depends. He might answer you right then or He might not give you clarity for a week, maybe longer."

"That's a problem."

"Why?"

"Besides the fact that CJ hates me—"

"That man could never hate you."

"Well, he's not exactly happy with me at the moment." Although, she knew her friend was right. He wasn't angry so much as he was hurt. Again. She'd broken his heart again. "And we have to work together."

"You survived before."

Only, this time would feel harder because Harper couldn't convince herself that they'd both moved on. "I also need to call that theater company back. They've already conducted their initial phone interviews and are starting in-person ones next week. Guess they hope to make a decision by month's end."

"Wow. They're not giving you much notice, are they?"

"Apparently, the man told his intern to contact me a month ago. He's not sure what happened but said when he never heard back, that he assumed I wasn't interested. Until he got a call from Chaz's mom."

"I see. Okay. Here's a truth I always find helpful when I want God to answer my prayer like yesterday. I remind myself that He wants me to know His will even more than I do, and He's always right on time. Never late, although He's rarely early, either."

"That's encouraging."

"Actually, it sort of is, once you understand why."

"Which is?"

"Because He wants you to trust Him, so that the next time you find yourself in a situation you're not sure how to handle, you won't freak out so much. This problem you're facing, and every problem you'll face every day after— they're nothing to Him. He's the all-powerful creator of the universe, after all. He holds all your—and Emaline's—tomorrows in His hands."

"Thanks, Trish. That really helps."

"My pleasure. Although you should realize

my advice doesn't come free. I bill in ice cream. Chocolate chip, one container, two spoons, and a night of chick flicks with my bestie."

"That, I will gladly pay."

She hung up, did an internet search for Little Tykes's number, then called.

Julia responded to her request to meet with audible skepticism. "Mind if I ask what about?"

Harper released a breath. She would've preferred to hold this conversation in person but assumed that wouldn't occur unless she gave Julia more info. She shared her idea.

"Intriguing." The caution in her tone evaporated. "We certainly have the ceiling for it."

"I remembered your big, strong beams."

"Let me give this some prayer and get back to you."

Harper frowned. "Sure, no problem." What if Julia didn't reply in time?

Trisha had said God was never late or early. Harper would simply have to trust that He would lead her when it was time for her to be led. And that He would make His guidance clear.

Pray, praise, then listen.

With a sigh, she turned on the radio and tapped Search until she found a Christian station. She didn't know the lyrics well enough to sing along, so instead, she turned onto a dirt road and parked beneath the shade of a mature oak.

Leaning against the headrest, she closed her eyes and let the music, which spoke of God's love and faithfulness, fill her mind and soul.

She must've fallen asleep, because she was jolted awake by the ringing of her phone. Sucking in a startled breath, she scanned her surroundings to orient herself. The sun was beginning to set, streaking the sky in gradient hues of pink, purple and red.

Her phone rang again and Emaline started to cry.

"I'm here, sweet pea." Reaching for her cell, she jumped out and slid in beside her daughter's car seat. The way Emaline rubbed her eyes indicated she was just waking up herself.

She answered. "Hello?" Phone sandwiched between her shoulder and ear, she unfastened Emaline and cradled her in her arms.

"Harper, this is Mrs. Jenkins. CJ's had an accident."

"What?" She felt dizzy as an image of CJ and his truck, upside down in some ditch, roof caved in, filled her mind. "What kind of accident?"

"Chain saw. That's all we know. We're headed to the hospital now."

He was alive! *Thank You, Lord Jesus.*

For now. There was no way to know until she arrived just how severe his injuries were. She'd read an article about a guy that had fallen on his blade, slicing it into his neck and shoulder blades, only one-quarter inch from his carotid artery.

She struggled for air.

Stop it. He could easily have cut his hand. She'd seen a guy at the competition who'd been missing two of his fingers, an unpleasant occurrence, no doubt, but certainly not life-threatening.

"I'll meet you there." Ending the call, she returned Emaline to her car seat. The baby immediately began to fuss.

"I know, sweet pea. Just a little longer, I promise." Throwing her car into Reverse, she sped back onto the main country road, tempering her almost uncontrollable desire to speed with the need to drive safe for Emaline's sake.

Please, Lord, let him be okay.

What if he didn't make it? She didn't want their last encounter to be the moment when she should have chosen him but hadn't.

When she arrived at the hospital, CJ's parents, Ken, and about half of Trinity Faith, Trisha included, were already in the waiting room.

Her friend met her with open arms. "I'll take the munchkin."

"Thank you." She rushed to where Nancy was pacing. "Is he okay?"

Mrs. Jenkins looked at her with teary eyes.

"The doctor said he cut his femoral artery. He's in surgery now."

"But he got here in time? He's going to be all right?"

Mr. Jenkins came up beside his wife. "He should be. Boy acted quick, made himself a tourniquet using his belt, and called his neighbor." He motioned to an older guy with angular shoulders sitting a few chairs away. "Thank the Good Lord the fella was in and just about to head to town. Said he drove down his potholed dirt road fast enough to knock his teeth out."

Nancy nodded. "If he'd had to call 9-1-1, the soonest the ambulance would've gotten to him would've been fifteen minutes. That's if they flew."

CJ could've died. If he had, Harper never would've recovered. She knew that now. As for having to choose between him and the open choreography position—there was no question.

She wanted CJ—if he'd still have her.

Chapter Fifteen

CJ pushed up in the bed, his brain foggy from the pain medication steadily dripping into his IV. His mom was working a crossword puzzle from the chair she'd pulled close, while his dad sat near the window, remote in hand. He'd been flipping through channels for the past ten minutes, evidence of his discomfort remaining stationary.

"You don't have to stay," CJ said.

His dad looked up and shrugged. "Don't got anywhere I need to be just yet."

That couldn't be true considering they'd left Ken to run the store. Then again, Nuts, Bolts and Boards couldn't be that busy given the number of people that had stopped by the hospital to see him today.

None of them Harper.

That hurt more than the wound in his leg. Then again, he hadn't exactly been kind or understanding the day before. Pastor Roger once said that true love always sought the other person's best, even when doing so felt hard and painful.

Based on that definition, if CJ really cared about Harper, he'd want her to chase her dreams. Even if that meant her leaving.

He closed his eyes as a fresh wave of heartache swept over him. *Lord, help me love her like that.* Because he knew there was no way he could do that in his own strength. Not if it meant losing her.

Someone knocked on the open door.

He looked up and struggled to push himself into a more upright position. "Harper."

"Mind if I come in?" Her voice sounded small. Timid.

"Of course."

She greeted his parents with one nod, "Ma'am. Sir," then continued to his bedside, opposite from where his mom sat. She bit her lip, clearly wanting to talk but hesitant to do so.

Had she made her decision? Surely Harper wouldn't tell him now, not with him lying there, attached to machines and tubes.

Then again, he never thought she'd leave him on the night of her graduation, either.

"How are you feeling?" Worry lines stretched across her forehead.

"About like I almost sliced my leg off." He

chuckled. "Just kidding. They've got me covered." He lifted his arm with the IV. "How are you?"

"Much better, now that I know you're okay." She blinked quickly, like she used to when she was fighting tears. "I, um…" She glanced first to his mom then his dad, then back to him.

"We were just leaving." His mom stood. "Isn't that right, Johnny?"

He frowned. "Were we going?"

"Come on." She grabbed his arm and pulled him out of the room with a backward wave and a cheery, "We'll be back. Good to see you, Harper."

"Yes, ma'am." She faced CJ again. "I'm really sorry about—"

"What? Getting a phone call? One that you've probably been waiting for since you arrived in Sage Creek?" He shook his head. "I'm the one who needs to apologize." He swallowed past a lump in his throat, not sure he had the strength to say what he knew he needed to. "I don't want to hold you back. I want to be the one person in your life that most encourages you to fly, and if that means moving to Portland, then I'm for that. Because I'm for you."

"That's not what I want." A tear slid down her cheek, and CJ wished he could reach her to wipe it away. To touch her face and run the pad of his thumb across her bottom lip. To feel her mouth on his once again, even if for the last time.

A flicker of hope ignited within him. "What are you saying?"

He was almost afraid to ask, because her answer could shatter him. Or flood his soul with joy he'd worried he might never experience again. Joy he couldn't experience apart from her.

"I don't want that job, or any job, if that means losing you." She grabbed his hand in both of hers. "Oh, CJ, when your mom called, I was so frightened. I worried you might not make it—"

"Death from a leg wound?" The corners of his mouth twitched toward a smile. "It's going to take a lot more than that to wipe me out."

Harper laughed and slapped his arm. "You're horrible. Seriously, CJ, I didn't know how badly you were hurt, and as I drove to the hospital, all I could think about was how empty my life would be without you. And how wonderful it has been to once again have you by my side. Although, I have to say, that wasn't exactly what I meant when I asked God to make His will clear!"

"What are you talking about?"

"Private joke."

"Between you and the Lord?"

"Something like that. On another, and much more important note, will you forgive me?"

His throat felt tight. "There's nothing to forgive."

Palming away her tears, she gave him a wobbly smile. "Does that mean you'll take me back?"

"Woman, I will hold tight to you for as long as you'll let me, and a thousand years beside." The ring! He still had the engagement ring in his pants.

He glanced around. Where had the hospital put his jeans? They hadn't thrown them away when they'd cut them off him, had they? Yes, he could buy another engagement ring, but it wouldn't be the same. He'd been saving that one—for her. Always for her.

Harper studied him. "What's wrong?"

"Can you hand me my phone?" He motioned to his bedside tray, which the nurse had wheeled out of the way.

"Uh. Sure." She grabbed it and gave it to him. "Did you need me to get you something?"

He shot his mom a text, asking about his clothing. "Nope. I mean, yeah, but…nope." The phone chimed his mom's response. She'd sent him three question marks.

Harper started to speak when his mom burst through the door. "What you needin' your pants for, boy?" She planted a fist on her hip. "If you're thinking about getting up and walking out of here, I'm here to tell you that is not happening.

Even if I got to get your dad to strap you to that bed."

Harper looked between them with a perplexed brow. "Pants?"

"Never mind." CJ shot his mom a pointed look.

She crossed her arms. "What?" Then, a look of understanding swept across her face, and she turned to Harper, nudging her toward the door in a similar fashion as she had his father. "I'm sorry, but CJ should probably get some rest. He's had a lot of visitors this morning."

Harper's eyebrows shot up. "Oh. Of course." Fingers rubbing her collarbone, she paused in the doorway to look back at CJ. "I'll call you?"

"Sure."

When she was gone, his mom turned to him with a frown. "What in the blazes was that about?"

"Do you know what happened to my clothes?"

"What clothes?"

"That I was wearing when I came in."

"Those are nothing but scraps, darling. But I can bring you something from your house. When they discharge you."

He told her about the ring.

"And you think this is the time and place to propose?" She swept an arm to indicate the hospital room.

"Seems perfect to me. What better way to celebrate that I'm alive—thank You, Jesus." He cast a glance to the ceiling. "Than grabbing hold of life with both hands?"

"You're afraid she'll change her mind?"

Was he? Maybe a little, but that was just his insecurity talking. "I've been waiting on that woman for going on six years now. Guess I'm tired of waiting. That said, I was hoping you'd help me with the proposal part."

"How so?"

"First, by helping me find the ring. I sure hope they didn't toss it."

"Nope. They gave me and Dad your stuff. It's still in the car. Want me to go get it? And your wallet, too?"

"That'd be great. Mind swinging by Blooming Bouquets for flowers and balloons? Use my credit card."

"Any particular type?"

"Red roses and balloons. Three hundred dollars' worth. Think Arlene would cut us a deal?" The florist and his mom had been friends since middle school.

"If I tell her why I'm buying them, she just might sell everything at cost. The biggest problem might be her not having enough for what you want." She tapped a finger to her chin. "How about I reach out to the Stoughtons?"

"Caden's folks?" They had a bee farm not far

out of town. Their property was a kaleidoscope of color.

She nodded. "Bet they'd give us about as many flowers as we can cut."

"That sounds like a lot of work and time."

"Not if I get the Trinity Faith gals to help. I'll shoot Lucy a text." She served on the town's cultural committee. "She'll probably have fifty ladies lined up by the time I reach Arlene's."

"Might want to call the Stoughtons first."

"Duh." She rolled her eyes. But then her expression sobered and tears glistened in her eyes. "I can't believe my son's going to get married."

"She has to say yes first."

She waved a hand. "You know what I mean." She turned to leave, then paused in the doorway. "Keep your phone handy. I'll probably be calling with a bazillion questions."

"I will. Although I'm pretty sure you and Arlene will know the answers before I do."

But there was only one answer he was concerned with, and only Harper could provide that.

Harper sat on her couch, trying to distract herself by playing with a puzzle app, but her thoughts kept replaying her visit with CJ. Why had he acted so strangely? And his mom, too. Had they been talking about her?

She didn't believe what Nancy had said about

CJ being tired. There had to have been another reason they'd wanted Harper to leave.

Emaline began to fuss from her crib.

Harper stood. "Coming, sweet girl."

She strolled down the hall and into the bedroom.

"Hey, there, sweet girl." Her daughter responded with a toothless smile as Harper slipped her arms under her and picked her up. "You want to snuggle with Mama for a bit?" She kissed her soft forehead, relishing her baby scent.

Diaper changed, she carried her daughter to the rocker purchased at a local garage sale. She loved these post-naptime moments when Emaline was alert and content to simply let Harper hold her.

Rocking, she began to sing the lyrics for a song she vaguely remembered from church, when her phone rang.

Was that CJ?

She stood, carrying Emaline, and hurried to the living room to where she'd left her phone on the coffee table. She didn't recognize the number.

"Hello?"

"Hi, this is Julia from Little Tykes."

"Yes?" A jolt of anticipation shot through her.

"I've been thinking and praying over your offer. I think you've got a great idea and I'm certain we could work together on times."

"You mean…?"

"I'd love to rent you space and, knowing how hard it is to get a new venture off the ground, I won't charge you for the first month."

"Wow. That's so generous, thank you! So, now what?"

"I expect you're going to hire a contractor to set everything up how you want it?"

"Yes, ma'am." CJ could help her with all that.

"Want to meet next week to talk details?"

"I'd love that."

Ending the call, she sank into the couch and bounced Emaline, standing on her thighs. "Grandma was right. Jesus is more than big enough to give me both of my dreams." Tears pricked her eyes. "Thank You, Lord."

She couldn't wait to tell CJ. She clicked to her contacts and hit Call.

"Hey." She could hear the smile in his voice. "I was just thinking about you."

"Yeah? Then why'd you kick me out?"

He chuckled. "I didn't kick you out."

"You kind of did. You going to tell me what all that was about?"

He paused. "Nope."

Why was he being so secretive? "You're making me nervous."

He laughed. "There's nothing to fret about."

"Did you get some rest?"

"I did, thanks. Feeling better by the hour."

"Wonderful. Does that mean you're up for visitors?"

Harper didn't know how to read his pause, especially since she could hear other voices in the background. "This evening, sure. Like, around five?"

"Okay."

She ended the call and sank, holding Emaline, into the couch.

He almost seemed reluctant to see her. He'd said he'd forgiven her, but had he really? Maybe he was more upset than he'd let on. Either that, or maybe his pain medication had started to wear off and his clearer thinking had refueled whatever anger she'd triggered.

Or his accident had simplified things for him, as it had for her; only, unlike her, he'd determined that she wasn't the one. And could she blame him? She didn't exactly have her life together, whereas his was finally taking off.

He'd been on television, won a lucrative award and a place in a prestigious gallery, had purchased building space, and would soon have his own business. One that, with his talent, wisdom and hard work ethic, was sure to succeed.

Tears stung her eyes. "I fear your grandma's warnings may have been right, Ema-bean. I think I may have lost CJ for good this time."

Moping about the house worrying for the next four hours wouldn't help any.

She stood. "How about we distract ourselves with a blended peppermint mocha and giant chocolate chip cookie from the Literary Sweet Spot and some downtown window-shopping? And maybe a stop at the library for some new bedtime stories for you and a novel for me."

Unfortunately, her desire not to obsess over CJ proved stronger than her ability. After a couple of hours, she gave up and hopped in her car. She arrived at the hospital nearly forty-five minutes earlier than CJ had requested.

She followed behind an older woman she recognized from Trinity Faith pushing a rolling cart of the most beautiful wildflowers in an assortment of vases. She was on the shorter side, with a boxy shape, and had long black hair that hit midback.

As they neared, the sliding glass doors swooshed open, releasing a gust of cold air and the scent of cleaner. When the woman struggled to push her cart over the door seal on the floor, Harper stepped forward.

"Let me help."

"Thank you, my dear. This thingamajig is heavier than it looks."

"I can imagine." Harper wheeled it inside, then stopped, jaw slack, to see so many ladies walking past the main desk, all carrying flowers or balloons. Most, if not all of them, attended Trinity Faith.

"Guess someone is well loved," she said to herself.

Lucy Carr, who'd been hurrying past from the other direction, overheard her and stopped with a grin and dancing eyes. "Oh, yes, I would say so." But then her expression flashed from surprise to concern. "Where are you going?"

"To see a friend."

Lucy's gaze shot down the hall then back to Harper. "Are you in a hurry? Because—"

"Harper!"

She turned at Nancy's alarmed voice, and her pulse immediately spiked. Had something happened to CJ? An unexpected infection or something? "Ma'am. Is everything all right?"

Nancy and Lucy exchanged looks, and neither appeared pleased by her presence. "Yes, of course. But…"

"I was just about to ask Harper if she'd mind helping me." Lucy's tone made it seem as if her words were laden with ulterior meaning.

"Oh, yes." Nancy brightened. "Great idea. I could use some help as well."

Why was everyone acting so strange all of a sudden? "With?"

"I'll show you." She placed a hand in the crook

of Harper's arm and gently rotated her back toward the door. "It's in my trunk."

"Mine, too." Lucy came alongside them, both women practically tugging Harper outside, only to seem completely baffled once they reached their vehicles.

But rather than admitting they didn't have whatever items they'd thought they'd brought, they spent the next ten minutes or so searching every inch of each of their vehicles. The back seat and front. The floorboard.

The glove compartment? Surely they could manage whatever could fit there on their own.

When they started talking about driving home to get their items, and it seemed as if they actually wanted Harper to accompany them, she politely excused herself and hurried back toward the hospital.

"Harper, wait." Nancy's footsteps approached quickly from behind.

Once inside, she turned to face her with a smile. "I would love to help you, ma'am. I can stop by your house in a couple hours. Or the store. Wherever."

Nancy released a breath and threw up her hands. "Never mind."

Great. She'd offended the woman. "I'm sorry. I wasn't trying to be rude."

"No, really, it's all right." She glanced at the

clock on the wall and then, with a much more relaxed smile, once again placed her hand in the crook of Harper's arm. "Let's go see how my son's doing, shall we?"

"Yes, ma'am."

Other women passed them, eyebrows shooting up upon seeing Harper, as they strolled down the hall. She couldn't help but feel as if they were all sending hidden messages to one another—about something she, apparently, was the only one to know nothing about.

Upon entering CJ's room, she stopped short, eyes wide. Vases, some filled with roses and others with bluebonnets, primroses, daisies, white poppies and other wildflowers, decorated literally every surface space and overflowed onto the floor. Among them were numerous balloons more fitting for Valentine's Day than any get-well sentiments.

CJ sat upright in his bed, cowboy hat on, grinning.

"You're certainly a popular man." Had he always been so, or was this the result of his contest placement and television appearance?

"Oh, I don't know about that."

"Because every hospital room looks like this?" She laughed. "You always did have a way of winning people's hearts."

"There's only one heart I'm interested in."

The women who'd been in the room when she'd arrived deposited their gifts and scurried out.

She shook her head. "Why is everyone acting so strange?"

"Come here." He shifted to make room beside him, his intensified gaze capturing hers.

Harper knew that look. She'd seen it before.

She came closer and sat on the edge of the mattress, angled toward him. She swallowed. "Christopher Jenkins, what are you doing?"

"What I meant to do years ago." He produced a black velvet box from beneath the blanket. "You have done grabbed hold of every last piece of my heart. You're constantly in my thoughts, and you and that adorable daughter of yours have invaded my dreams."

She quirked an eyebrow, her pulse ricocheting against her breastbone. "Invaded, huh?"

He nodded. "Grabbed hold of every last one. Back when we were teens, I thought there was no way I could possibly love you more, but I was wrong. What I felt then, as powerful as that was, pales in comparison to the way I feel about you now. I don't want to spend a single day without you."

A tear slid down her face as CJ opened the box and took out the ring.

He grabbed her trembling hand in his and

slipped a gold band with a glimmering diamond bordered by tiny pink sapphires onto her finger. "Harper, will you make me the happiest man alive, from now until I breathe my last, by marrying me?"

"Oh, CJ! Yes!"

His eyes and grin widened. But then his expression sobered as he cupped her face in both his hands, leaned in close and seized her lips in his.

Feeling as if her chest would burst, she grasped the back of his neck, breathing in his smell and his taste as he deepened his kiss.

God had indeed given her both of her dreams.

Behind them came a muffled, "Praise God Almighty!"

Releasing her hold, she glanced back to see the faces of the Trinity Faith ladies pressed up against the hall window and poking through the open door, Nancy's bright eyes among them.

Harper laughed and shook her head. "What's that saying about news traveling fast in small towns?"

CJ shot her the easy grin that always turned her insides to mush. "Guess some things don't change, huh?"

"And I hope they never will."

Epilogue

One year later

"Now, don't you look scrumptious." Harper's mom lifted Emaline, dressed in ballet shoes, a pink leotard with embroidered flowers and a matching tutu, and twirled her about the parish house's living room. "It's really not fair to all the other ballerina flower girls, you're so cute."

Harper laughed. "I'm just glad she's not fighting to take her outfit off. I can't tell you how many times I heard 'Itchy, Mama' when I got her dressed."

"I'm sure seeing the bigger kids in the same getup helped."

"She does want to be grown, that's for sure."

"Reminds me of someone else at her age." Her mom kissed Emaline's cheek then set her down. She turned to Harper. "And you, my girl, look absolutely beautiful." Eyes glistening, she took hold of both of her hands. "Just wait until CJ sees you. He's liable to fall over flat."

"Thank you." Harper turned toward the mirror and ran a hand down the bodice of her form-fitting, boho gown. White fabric decorated with cherry blossoms over pink satin formed the silhouette. The tips of her shoes, clear sandals with white flowers, peeked out from beneath the fabric.

"He might fall over before he even gets to that point, with how nervous he's been this morning." Nancy, who'd slipped in with a white basket filled with chilled water bottles, shot Harper a wink. "Can't say I blame him. He's been waiting for this day—for his lady—for an awful long time."

Harper's heart swelled to think of how faithfully he'd loved her, even when she'd spurned his love. "I'm very grateful."

"You realize what that means, right?" Nancy grabbed a tissue and dabbed at her glistening forehead, evidence of all the running around she'd been doing. Everyone had insisted, numerous times, that she relax and simply enjoy the day, but her obvious nervousness wouldn't let her.

"What's that?" Harper fingered her necklace, a crystal teardrop hung on a silver chain.

"He won't let you go, no how, no way."

He'd well proven that.

"Not you or Little Ms. Twinkle Toes." Nancy glanced around. "Where are the other dancers?"

"With Trisha and Julia, getting warmed up. And probably receiving an earful of directions."

A gentle knock sounded on the door and, a moment later, Lucy, who'd worked tirelessly—with the help of her friends—on the decorations, using a plethora of wildflowers donated by the Stoughtons, poked her head inside. "Y'all about ready?"

Harper took a deep breath and nodded. "As ready as I'll ever be."

"And the others?"

"I'll get them." Her mom dashed into the living room, her anxious voice following.

A moment later, half a dozen of Harper's dance students, aged three to five, burst into the kitchen, her mom shooing them forward.

Trisha and Julia trailed behind, radiant in their matching off-the-shoulder bridesmaid dresses, their hair secured by the same beaded pins as Harper's.

With another quick yet firm knock, CJ's dad entered, wearing a suit, perhaps for the second time in his life, the first being his wedding. Upon seeing Harper, he stopped short then gave a low whistle. "My boy sure snagged him a good one."

His wife slapped his arm.

He laughed and came to Harper's side. "Joking aside, he done did good. You still okay with me walking you down the aisle?"

A lump lodged in her throat. A year ago, she never would've imagined it would be CJ's dad walking her down the aisle. It had touched her deeply when he'd offered, and had helped lessen the ache left by her uninvolved father.

Both of CJ's parents had been amazing, opening their hearts to her as if she were their own daughter. "I wouldn't want anyone else to."

She would've been overjoyed, simply to wed a man like CJ Jenkins. Yet God in His abundance had given her an added gift in allowing her to marry into such a wonderful family.

CJ took a deep breath, his legs jittery, as the music started. It was the instrumental version of a song about a couple reunited after a long separation who remained together through life's ups and downs, wrinkles and gray hair. His chest squeezed with the same intensity as it had when Harper had first played it for him—his thoughts immediately spanning the years that lay before them.

When he'd lost her that first time, he wasn't sure he could go on. The hurt had felt so intense, he'd wanted to close his heart for good. Praise God he hadn't, otherwise he would've missed out on the best gift Christ had ever given him.

Heads turned and people gasped as a handful of girls dressed in leotards and tutus, their hair secured in matching buns, pranced up the aisle on tiptoes, dropping petals as they went. His princess followed, led by the hand by yet another dancer. At eighteen months, she was looking more like her mother every day, and had captured his heart as securely.

God help me do right by that girl. Be the type of dad she needs, and the husband Harper deserves.

Nearing the altar, Emaline noticed CJ, and a wide grin lit her face. "Daddy!" She yanked free from her guide, dropped her petal basket and hurriedly toddled toward him.

He laughed and scooped her up. "Hey, peanut." He kissed her cheek. "What a great dancer you are!"

Expression serious, she nodded. "My toe-toes." She pointed to her lifted foot.

"On your tiptoes. I saw." With a gentle squeeze, he placed her in his mother's waiting arms.

The music shifted, this time to the song he'd chosen about a woman so beautiful, inside and out, her man frequently lost his ability to think and speak. A woman whose laugh sounded like the notes from a flute and whose smile lit a room. A woman with an elegant grace and tender touch who made the singer want to be a better man.

A woman like Harper.

His breath caught as she emerged around the corner, looking more gorgeous than he'd ever seen her, in a gown that accentuated her delicate frame. Her hair cascaded over her shoulders, jewels of some sort glimmering throughout the strands.

When she drew near, he noted the shimmer of her lip gloss, the soft pink in her cheeks and the curve of her lashes around her sapphire eyes.

Reaching him, she handed Trisha, her bridesmaid, her bouquet, and faced him with a shy smile that triggered a gut-level protectiveness within him. The part of him that would do anything in his power to make her happy.

Pastor Roger motioned for everyone to sit, thanked them for coming, then talked about a love so deep, it revealed the depth of love Christ had for each of us, which in turn equaled the love the Father and Son had for one another. He then indicated for CJ to say his vows.

He wiped sweaty hands on his pant legs and pulled out his sheet of paper. Unfolding it, he cleared his throat. "Harper Moore, I can still picture the day I first saw you, sitting on my neighbor's back porch, holding a fussing baby in your arms. The way your brow furrowed, and how your wavy hair framed your face. How your eyes lit up a moment later when you laughed at something one of the other kids had said. I knew then that you were a rare treasure worth cherishing."

CJ swallowed, his nervousness giving way to a rush of emotion. "When you left for Seattle, I feared I'd lost you for good. And that I'd never get over you, no matter how hard or long I tried. I was right. I didn't, and I never will. You and that wiggly, giggly, twinkle-toed peanut make life worth living. I thank God each day for bringing you back to me. Now that He has, there's no way I'll ever let you go."

A tear slid down Harper's cheek and she palmed it away. "Nor I you, CJ Jenkins. That girl who left all those years ago was a fool. Because if she'd had a clue as to the gift she'd been given—the type of person you are—she would've realized no dream is worth losing you. You're a man of integrity, of gentleness and strength, who's the first to give, the first to help, and the first—and last—to capture my heart, which I freely give, without hesitation or reservation."

Her words reached the deepest place within him where a hint of insecurity still resided, not because of anything she'd done, but rather because he knew how far out of his league she was.

"You've both spoken powerful words I have no doubt you'll live out in the years to come," Pastor Roger said before directing them to exchange rings. "And now, by the power vested in me by the State of Texas, I pronounce you husband and wife. Christopher James Jenkins, you may now kiss your bride."

A grin exploded across his face then evaporated as his eyes locked onto hers. Cupping her cheeks in his hands, he brought his lips to hers, almost heady with the realization that he'd be kissing this beautiful woman a thousand times a day for the rest of his life.

* * * * *

If you liked this story from Jennifer Slattery, check out her previous Love Inspired books:

Falling for the Family Next Door
Her Small-Town Refuge
Chasing Her Dream

Available now from Love Inspired!
Find more great reads at
www.LoveInspired.com.

Dear Reader,

Every town has that one thing—a restaurant, fountain or business—that features prominently in most everyone's memories. Perhaps it's a barbecue restaurant where teenagers have been hanging out for decades. Maybe it's a lake at which most every family spends the majority of their summer. Or perhaps it's a family-owned hardware store that has supplied homeowners with material and information they used to build, repair and remodel their house in which they formed precious memories.

That is what Meeske Hardware store means to the community of Weeping Water, Nebraska. As I researched *Recapturing Her Heart* and heard the love and admiration Weeping Water residents expressed for the Meeske family and their store, I knew I wanted Nuts, Bolts and Boards to have a similar feel and play an equally important role in the lives of Sage Creek residents. Because every town needs a Meeske's. I would love to hear your "Meeske" story! You can connect with me at jenniferaslattery@gmail.com or through my website at JenniferSlatteryLivesOutLoud.com.

Much love!
Jennifer